Dear Reader,

I'm delighted that *Summer After Summer* is being reissued. Although this story is purely a figment of my imagination, writing it reminded me of my teenage years in Seguin, Texas—back when I could still wear a bikini and sun worshipping was cool. And yep—we did have our own version of the Pink Pig.

Have you ever fantasized about running into your first love? Tell the truth—in that daydream you're trim, slim and heart-stoppingly gorgeous. Not so for Jazzy Rinaldi, my heroine in *Summer After Summer*. When she encounters Charlie Morrison in the wine aisle at the grocery store, she's well past shabby chic—not to mention she's also premenopausal and has a kid who covets a belly-button ring. That's the stuff of nightmares.

In this story, Jazzy and Charlie prove that love can survive long separations, family crises and (most traumatic of all) a high school reunion. Their story confirms there's love, laughter and great times after fifty. I adore these characters and I hope you enjoy them as much as I did creating them.

Guadalupe County, Texas, is a self-proclaimed pecan capital. There's even a gigantic replica of a pecan on the courthouse lawn to prove it. So this recipe seems perfect. Forget the calories and enjoy!

PECAN PIE

3 eggs
1 cup sugar
1 tbsp flour
1 tbsp butter, melted
1 cup corn syrup
1 cup pecan halves
1 unbaked piecrust

Beat eggs, adding sugar gradually, with flour and melted butter. Add syrup, stirring to mix well. Add pecans, stirring to coat. Pour into unbaked piecrust. Bake at 450° F for 10 minutes. Reduce oven to 350° F and bake for 40 minutes or until center is firm.

Ann

P.S. I love hearing from my readers. My address is P.O. Box 266, Lightfoot, VA 23090-0266. My email address is adefee@cox.net. And don't forget to visit my website at www.ann-defee.com.

ABOUT THE AUTHOR

Ann DeFee's debut novel, *A Texas State of Mind* (Harlequin American Romance), was a double finalist in the 2006 Romance Writers of America's prestigious RITA® Award contest. *Summer After Summer* won a 2008 Book Buyers' Best award for Series Long Contemporary.

Drawing on her background as a fifth-generation Texan, Ann loves to take her readers into the sassy, and sometimes wacky, world of a small Southern community. As an air force wife with twenty-three moves under her belt, she's now settled in Williamsburg, Virginia, and loving all the opportunities of living in the epicenter of American history. When she's not writing, you might find her exploring the colonial, Revolutionary War and Civil War historic sites abundant in Virginia.

Books by Ann DeFee

Other titles by this author available in ebook format.

Summer After Summer

ANN DeFEE

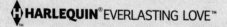
HARLEQUIN®EVERLASTING LOVE™

Recycling programs
for this product may
not exist in your area.

ISBN-13: 978-0-373-22969-7

SUMMER AFTER SUMMER

Printed in U.S.A.

Summer After Summer

This book is dedicated to Paula Eykelhof,
who believed in this story
and has championed all the wonderful books
of the Everlasting line.

Summer 1973

Chapter 1

"Jasmine Boudreaux! You girls watch out for snakes now, ya hear?" Mama's honeyed drawl drifted over the languid green river to the wooden raft where I was sunbathing with my three best friends—Bunny Bennett, Mary Alice Cunningham and Misty Stewart.

Although we were as different as the four points of the compass, we'd been best buddies since our first day in kindergarten. Mary Alice was thoughtful, sensitive and more than a little religious. Bunny, the wild child, was on the opposite end of the spectrum. And Misty was our version of intelligentsia, bouncing back and forth between arcane ideologies. One day you'd find her quoting Ayn Rand; the next she'd be reading Karl Marx.

And speaking of dichotomies—I was a walking, talking Gemini. Although I was the most pragmatic member of our group, I was naive enough to fall for every practical joke in the universe.

I was fairly sure Mary Alice and I were the only two virgins in our senior class. I say that tentatively because virginity, or lack of it, was one of the few things we didn't discuss.

"Bucky said he saw at least half a dozen moccasins in the river last night, and you know how those nasty things like to get up on that old dock to sun."

"Yes, Mama, we'll be careful," I replied, although I didn't bother to open my eyes. Through some strange quirk of fate, Bucky was my brother. He was a junior at the University of Texas and he was absolutely positive he was the grand pooh-bah of the Western world. Truth be told, he was a pain in the rear.

Bunny sat up and engaged Mama in conversation—an exceptionally bad idea since my mother loved to talk.

"Miz Boudreaux, did my mom call?" Bunny could put on the thickest Texas accent you ever heard. And this was one of those occasions.

"No, honey, she hasn't. What do you want me to tell her if she does?" Mama had to yell in order to be heard.

"Just remind her I'm spending the night here, if you would. Not that she really cares where I am." That last sentence was meant strictly for our ears.

"Sure thing, honey," Mama agreed. "Jazzy, we're eating at the country club so you girls go to the Pink Pig for supper. I'll leave some money on the kitchen table."

In Meadow Lake, Texas, population 8,631, the Pink Pig Burger Emporium was the "happening" place. "Happening," that is, if you were into junk food, teenagers and the occasional redneck—"happening," of course, being a relative term.

Growing up in a small south Texas town when your daddy's the police chief presented some challenges. Everyone, and I do mean everyone, thought it was their job to report my every move. Swear to goodness, if I'd been audacious enough to utter the f-word, Mama would've known about it before I closed my mouth.

Every weekend, the kids had this ritual where we all circled the Pink Pig, cruised to the park on the other side of town, came back around to check out the movie theater, swung by Garcia's Pizzeria and then completed the circuit with a trip back to the PP. Round and round we went in a relentless circle of teenage hormones.

I was so busy thinking about life in the high-school zone that I almost missed the fact that Mama was still dispensing advice from the shore.

"Misty, you watch out and don't get sunburned. With your red hair, you could blister right up." Mama was well into her drill-sergeant routine.

"Yes, ma'am," the redhead in question yelled as she rolled over and smeared more baby oil on her exposed stomach. "Maybe if I get my freckles to run together I'll be able to tan. What do ya think?" she asked, even though we all knew it was a rhetorical question.

Misty had been trying to tan since the fourth grade and she'd never progressed beyond the burn, peel and freckle stage. I, on the other hand, had the skin of my Cajun ancestors and by the end of the summer I was as brown as a berry. It was one of those things that made her crazy.

One of the benefits of living in a small town was that you could have lifelong friends. We'd shared everything—our thoughts, our dreams and on occasion our communicable diseases. The only exception to the "share and share alike" rule was boyfriends. But that's a story I'll get to later.

Bunny's dad owned a tractor factory, which employed half the people in town. She was our bouncy blonde. The bouncy part came naturally; the blondeness was courtesy of a bottle.

The Bennetts were filthy rich and loved to flaunt it. Mrs. Bennett's diamonds rivaled the crown jewels. And that marble mausoleum Bunny called home was totally sterile.

Misty's parents were professors. They had to be book smart or they wouldn't be teaching at the college. However, I thought their general IQ was questionable. Sometimes they treated their only child as if she'd just popped in from another planet.

Mary Alice was a total sweetheart. A bit clueless in the fashion department, but one of the nicest people you could meet. Her dad was a Holy Roller preacher—need I say more?

So now you have an idea why we spent so much time at my house. My parents were cool, most of the time anyway, plus we had a ski boat. And for some unfathomable reason Misty had a major-league crush on Bucky. Just thinking about Misty and Bucky doing anything erotic exceeded my yuck factor.

We were freshly minted high-school graduates and feeling invincible. Actually, that wasn't quite the truth, at least for me. I was terrified. In a moment of insanity I'd applied to the school of architecture at U.C.

Berkeley—that's in California—and to my amazement I was accepted. It seemed like a good idea when I was filling out the application, but California, good grief!

What *was* I thinking?

"Jazzy! You're daydreaming again." Misty put her thumb over the lip of her Coke bottle and pretended to spray me. "I have a rumor to spread."

"Wow," the rest of the group said in chorus. Misty was usually the last person to hear anything. Not that she was ditzy; she just didn't pay much attention to gossip.

"My mother was on the phone talking to Dean Patrick. She was whispering, but I got the drift of the conversation. Sandy Sorenson is getting married. Her daddy's on the faculty, you know." She paused for dramatic effect. "Sandy *has* to get married!"

"Sandy Sorenson," Mary Alice whispered. "Oh, my God, she is *so* beautiful."

Sandy was in her freshman year at the University of Texas, and rumor had it she'd taken the campus by storm.

"Who's the guy?" Not that I was prone to

telling tales, but I figured we might as well get all the facts.

"I don't know. When Mom saw me she went into the laundry room and closed the door." Misty frowned. "Isn't it awful that Sandy has to get married?"

Her comment sent me into my women's lib mode. "Why would anyone 'have' to get married in this day and age? Please!" Talk about making me crazy. We weren't living in the 1950s. *I Love Lucy* and its archaic view of sex was nothing more than a TV rerun.

I was about to continue my rant when I noticed that Bunny was curiously silent. Usually she was the first to jump in on a good story.

Mary Alice piped up instead. "A baby needs parents who are married."

Our sweet little friend was getting annoyed. Normally she was fairly open-minded, but on the topic of babies and pregnancy her church background came to the fore.

"Billy Tom said he's ready for tonight," Bunny commented. That girl was the queen of the non sequitur, and this was a subject that definitely needed to be changed.

So Sandy Sorenson took a backseat while we discussed our upcoming adventure. Although it took some world-class wheedling, we'd finally convinced our buddy Billy Tom to help us get drunk for the first time. As a group, we had a well-earned reputation for being "Goody-Two-Shoes"—no booze and no pot. Since we were all heading to college, we decided to take a walk on the wild side… in a safe environment. And you couldn't get much safer than being with Billy Tom. It wasn't so much that he was benign; it was the fact that we had a ton of blackmail material on him.

"He paid some guy five bucks to buy us three six-packs. That's four apiece." Bunny was our soiree coordinator. "I'm not sure any of us will be coherent after four beers."

Neither was I, but I was certainly no expert. Most of the kids went out to the river to drink and neck and God only knows what else. Daddy was well aware of the kegger parties and periodically sent a deputy to patrol the area. Needless to say, I had *never* attended one. If my daddy had caught me there, I would've been grounded until I qualified for social security, and that wasn't in my game plan. I had people to see and places to go.

"What did you tell Charlie we were doing tonight?" Mary Alice directed her question to Bunny. She was referring to Bunny's boyfriend who was, unfortunately, the love of my life. But that was a secret I wasn't about to share with anyone, not even my best friends, or to be more specific, *especially* not my best friends. Charlie, darn his hide, treated me like his buddy.

Charlie Morrison and Bunny had been a couple for almost a year, and in my opinion it was an ill-fated liaison. The Bennetts despised him, more than likely because he wasn't rich and his family wasn't socially prominent.

When Bunny and Charlie first started going out, her parents made the mistake of issuing an ultimatum, which was like waving a red flag at a bull. Tell the girl she couldn't do something, and she went full steam ahead. So all year she used her friends as an excuse to get out of the house.

I'd known Charlie's parents almost my entire life and I thought they were fantastic. They owned a fishing camp/restaurant down the road from our house. Looking back, I suppose it was little more than a beer joint but Mrs. Morrison's Friday Night hush puppies and fried catfish bash was famous throughout the county.

I'll never forget when I met the Morrison twins. It was my first day of school and Mama made a huge production about me riding the school bus. That was also the day Bubba Hawkins decided to make my life a living hell.

To give it a nice spin, he was a big, fat bully, and like all tyrants he homed in on the vulnerable. What he hadn't expected was Charlie Morrison. After Charlie and Colton, his fraternal twin, got through with Bubba he never bothered me again. That was the day I fell in love with Charlie.

When we were in elementary school, the Morrison twins and I spent most of our summer days playing cops and robbers in the pecan orchard by the river. Colton was a great buddy, but even then I knew Charlie was special.

It seemed like my entire life consisted of a collage of Charlie memories. He risked life and limb teaching me to water-ski—I wasn't the most coordinated person in the world. And when I got my learner's permit, he instructed me in the art of driving a stick shift. Again, a scary proposition.

But it was in the pecan orchard on a sultry summer night after our freshman year that he truly stole my heart. That was my first kiss, and what a kiss it was. My life would never be the same. Too bad the feeling wasn't reciprocated. Darn it, the idiot never kissed me again!

"I told him I was busy. He got all snotty. He'll just have to deal with it. It's not like we're joined at the hip," Bunny groused.

If Charlie wanted to stick to *me* like glue, I'd have been a happy, happy girl. But he was a passion I needed to ditch because obviously it didn't have a chance in *H-E*-double toothpicks of going anywhere. We were another Romeo and Juliet, except Romeo wasn't enamored of Juliet.

So there I was, a seventeen-year-old virgin (in more ways than one) planning to sneak off to the drive-in with a bunch of girls to slurp suds. And we were going to pull off this great misadventure in Billy Tom's '57 Plymouth that didn't even have a working radio.

How pitiful was that?

Chapter 2

"Shake a leg, you guys!" Bunny commanded. We were doing our hair and makeup while she was issuing orders. That girl was Simon Legree in a Shirley Temple body.

Misty's head was on the ironing board while Mary Alice tried to press her friend's long curly hair into submission.

"I hate you, you know that." Misty was referring to my Cher hair that was long, straight and very black.

"Tough titty said the kitty, but the milk's still good," I retorted. "At least you have boobs." A good offense makes the best defense.

"Enough of that!" Bunny yelled. When *had* she started taking lessons from Mama? "We have to get going or we'll miss Billy Tom." She was on a roll. "We'll take my car to the Pink Pig and he'll pick us up there."

Bunny had a cool red VW convertible. We loved to cruise around town in that baby. I had a rusty Ford station wagon and Misty and Mary Alice were sans wheels.

The Pink Pig was situated so you could drive in a circle around the building. Bunny made one perfunctory loop, but it was early so our audience was limited. Darn it! She parked under the awning next to one of the speakers and punched the call button. Did I mention we had the top down for maximum exposure?

"Can I take your order?" A tinny voice came from the speaker.

"Four burgers, four orders of fries, two Cokes, a Dr Pepper and a chocolate shake," Bunny answered, pushing the off button. Then she made a face at me. "I think it's disgusting that you can drink milk shakes and never gain an ounce."

"It's one of the few advantages of being tall enough to play with the Boston Celtics," I said. Much to my chagrin I was almost five feet ten inches, stick skinny and as flat as a board. In fact, I could stand sideways behind a telephone pole and you wouldn't see me. Why I ran around with three curvy, baby ballerinas was beyond me.

"Jazzy, Jazzy!"

"Oh, God, it's Petey, the band geek. Whatever you do, don't you dare call him over here." Mary Alice slid down in her seat.

Petey had a massive crush on Mary Alice. Unfortunately, she thought the poor guy was a dork.

I wasn't very good at obeying commands so I ignored her. "Hey, Petey, how's it hangin'?"

True, Petey Renfro was a band geek, but he was also my good friend. I was the drum major and he played a tuba that was almost as big as he was. People said we looked like Mutt and Jeff. So what? He made me laugh, and best of all he was my sidekick on band trips.

He scurried over to the car and vaulted into the backseat. Out of the corner of my eye, I could see that Mary Alice had slipped farther down in the front.

"My cousin's coming to town tomorrow and I'm having a pool party. Please say you'll come. We're doing it out on our patio and the Pink Pig's gonna cater," he cajoled.

Petey's mom was the party diva of Meadow Lake, so without a doubt the get-together would be a blast.

"You guys are invited, too," he casually told my friends. His cavalier attitude toward Mary Alice didn't fool me for a minute. Petey was counting on me to drag her along. Unreciprocated love flat-out sucked, and I considered myself an expert on the subject.

We had to lie through our teeth to get rid of Petey when Billy Tom finally cruised by to pick us up. Although B.T. drove one of the funkiest cars in town and it was awfully hard to miss, we didn't have much choice. He was probably the only person we could coerce into assisting us with our little adventure, and we were smart enough to know we had to have a *sober* driver.

So we ditched Bunny's car at the back of the parking lot and piled into B.T.'s junkmobile. Our blackmail material on him was really juicy. That boy wasn't about to squeal, not if he knew what was good for him.

Considering it was Friday night, privacy at the drive-in was at a premium. Although the parking lot was a sea of cars, I'm sure there weren't more than ten people actually watching the movie.

Wonder what everyone else was doing?

The minute Billy Tom pulled the Plymouth into a spot on the back row he started complaining. What the hell was he doing? His old man was gonna kill him. Jazzy's dad would throttle him. God, he'd be dead before he even got to graduate.

"Good Lord, Billy Tom. You're more nervous than a cat in a room full of rocking chairs. Chill out," I ordered. Whining was one of my pet peeves—especially when the whiner was a six-foot-two-inch wide receiver on the football team.

"If my folks find out about this, my ass will be grass and my old man'll be a power mower," he moaned. "I don't know why I let you talk me into something this stupid."

How about because we could manipulate him? "Don't worry, no one's gonna find out, so shut up and hand over the beer," I ordered. For some reason I was feeling brave. In unison we each took a can and popped the top.

Misty was the first to take a sip. She spit it out almost before it hit her mouth. "This stuff tastes like cat piss!"

It took a lot to rile up Billy Tom, but her comment did the trick. "You guys didn't give me enough money to get the good stuff. And they're hot 'cause I don't have a cooler! You're damn lucky you have me to drive you around," he mumbled.

"Don't worry about it, we'll drink them anyway." Mary Alice used her most soothing voice. That's what I loved about her; she was always a peacemaker.

And drink them we did. By the time I was halfway through the first can, the taste started to be tolerable. The second one was pretty good and after I finished the third, I was the brewski queen of south Texas. Oops! On the fourth, my nose went numb.

"I can't feel my nose." I was trying to act serious, but a bout of giggles ruined the effect. Fortunately, we were all happy drunks. Everything was hysterically funny. Then we began to sing. Bunny and Misty were cheerleaders, so they led us in multiple renditions of the school fight song. They even knew the third and fourth verses.

We were making so much noise they could've heard us in the next county. So much for discretion. That's when the dog doo hit the fan. I knew we were in a pile of trouble when Charlie Morrison jerked open the car door.

"What's going on?" He didn't shout and somehow that made his question more ominous.

"Angelique!" That was Bunny's real name, but Charlie was the only one who could get away with calling her that. "Get out of the car. What do you think you're doing?"

Although Bunny hadn't had as much to

drink as I had, she didn't appear to be in any condition to tell anyone anything. So I did what any good friend would do. I elegantly removed myself from the front seat—okay, I did a face plant, but I recovered nicely—and went toe to toe with Charlie.

"We're just having a few drinks." I might've been able to pull it off if I hadn't ended the sentence with a hiccup.

Charlie raced fast boats and competed in water ski-jumping contests. He was tall, tan, blond and lanky. Plus, he had the most gorgeous green eyes I'd ever seen. Everyone agreed that when he grew into his body he'd be heart-stopping, drool-inducing, movie-star handsome. I already thought he was. And did I mention I was head over heels in love with him?

"Jazzy, I'm disappointed in you. I figured you had better sense than to get involved in this kind of shenanigan."

Uh-oh, usually he called me Sunshine. And when had he perfected that school-principal glare? Enough was enough. He wasn't my daddy, and he sure wasn't my boyfriend—damn it!

"I thought you were seventeen, not thirty-seven," I retorted. "Where do you get off telling us what to do?" I was getting louder with every word, and by the time I finished my rant we'd acquired a substantial audience.

"Get back in the car." He gently pushed me toward the open door. "B.T., you haven't been drinking, have you?"

"Nope."

"Why don't you give me your keys? Colton will take you home."

Colton had joined the crowd and was standing around gawking. Who could blame him? We were creating quite a spectacle. Billy Tom evacuated that car like his pants were on fire, throwing Charlie his keys on the way out.

"I'm going to drive these nitwits home," Charlie said.

"Nitwits, I'll give you nitwits." I was itching for a fight.

But instead of taking me on, he laughed. "Get back in the car, Sunshine. You're going home."

Did I mention that unreciprocated love sucks?

It took me all of three minutes to get over being mad, and then we continued our group giggle all the way to the river. There's probably nothing worse than being stuck in a car with a bunch of tipsy teenage girls, but Charlie soldiered on.

"Oh, my God! I'm gonna pee my pants," Misty exclaimed. She was laughing so hard that tears were pouring down her face. Her comment wasn't terribly funny, but at the time I thought it was hysterical.

As we drew near my house, Charlie cut the lights and the engine. He didn't want my daddy to catch us. He'd always had the tendency to be the knight on the white horse, the protector of the young, the weak, the stupid.

We rolled through the gates and stopped under a low-hanging bougainvillea. Fortunately, we were spending the night in the guesthouse so there was at least a fifty-fifty chance we wouldn't wake up my parents.

"I think I'm gonna be sick." Misty put

her hand over her mouth and lunged for the door.

We all leaned out to watch Misty retch. The fragrant night air suddenly reeked of recycled Lone Star and Pink Pig burgers.

"Oh, crap. I'm puking petals," Misty squealed as she stared at the disgusting puddle by her feet.

We were so busy watching Misty that we missed the newest arrival. When I heard that voice I knew we were busted.

"What's going on out here?" It was Bucky—my sanctimonious, pain-in-the-butt brother.

"I'm puking petals," Misty announced. It was not one of her finer moments.

"Don't be stupid. That stuff came from the bougainvillea," he said, pointing to the flowers hovering over us. For some unknown reason, Bunny and I decided that was especially hilarious. The next round of giggles left us rolling in the grass.

Charlie and Bucky were *not* amused. When I finally got myself under control and glanced up, they were standing over us like a couple of condescending guardian angels.

I still can't believe I reverted to a grade-school mentality, but I did with a vengeance. I stuck out my tongue and came up with the pithiest comment I could, considering I had a beer-soaked brain.

"And a nanny, nanny, pooh, pooh to you, too."

It was immature and stupid; however, I did get in the last word.

So there!

Chapter 3

"Oh, my God! I'm dying." My head was in the toilet so I wasn't sure anyone heard me. "I'm puking my guts out," I wailed.

"Here," Bunny said, handing me a bottle of Coke. "This'll make you feel better."

"Nothing will make me feel better." At least nothing short of a permanent adios, and I wasn't ready for that. I flopped on the cold linoleum floor. "Why are *you* so perky?"

Her answering smile was enough to make me want to deck her.

"I didn't drink that much."

"Yeah, well." I was on the verge of coming up with a great answer, really I was, but my brain short-circuited when my tummy did another barrel roll.

"You'd better get well, PDQ. If you back out on going to the party, you're dead meat," Bunny threatened.

"Yew!" Why did she have to mention dead meat? Or any kind of meat, for that matter?

It took a six-pack of Cokes and a sleeve of saltines before I truly thought I could make it through the day. Now I was at Bunny's house doing what I did best—providing cover for my friend.

"You know your sneaking around is gonna to get us both in trouble," I griped as Bunny searched the bottom of her closet. "If your parents catch you going out with Charlie when they specifically told you not to, you'll be grounded for life. And if by some miracle you get out of the house before you're twenty-one, they'll never let you see me again."

Bunny seemed oblivious to my complaints as she continued to look for something. When that girl got focused on a goal, she got focused. And her single-mindedness always seemed to get me in trouble.

"Here it is," she crowed triumphantly, holding up a Scarlett O'Hara corset, minus the laces.

"What do you mean, here it is?" I was lounging on the bed getting a really bad feeling about this. But I consoled myself with the fact that I was bigger than she was, and I could overpower her if push came to shove.

"I found this in my mother's closet." She waved the offending piece of lingerie in my direction. "I know, I know. You don't wear a bra. But for tonight, you're gonna be the sex goddess of south Texas. We're doing a makeover."

"Like hell," I snorted. "You're not about to get me into that thing. It couldn't be more than a size two and I'm a ten."

"Size is not a problem. And yes, you are going to wear it. Since we're leaving from here, you won't have to sneak past the Baptist brigade."

She was referring to my parents—pillars of the Baptist church and ardent opponents of anything that smacked of sexy.

"So get this on while I find the dress I have in mind. Just you wait till I get you all dolled up!" She tossed the instrument of torture at me.

Did Bunny really believe I'd strip down and put that thing on? "No way. I'm perfectly happy in my current state." Unfortunately, my resolve wasn't nearly as tough as Bunny's, and eventually I capitulated. Darn it! I needed to work on my backbone.

"Hold your breath. I've almost got the hooks done up." She was pulling and tugging to fasten me into the Merry Widow.

Poor, poor Scarlett. I suspect the infamous Southern belle was a bitch because her corset had restricted the flow of blood to her brain.

"Stay right there while I get this sundress on you," Bunny instructed, holding up an emerald-green, low-cut dress with spaghetti straps. After she waved the little scrap of material, she turned me away from the mirror.

"I can't wear your clothes. I'm at least eight inches taller than you are, and I'm at least twenty pounds heavier."

Now that was something I hated to admit.

"Exactly," Bunny said smugly as she yanked the dress over my head and somehow managed to get it zipped. She put her hands on her hips and circled me.

"Don't you dare look in the mirror," she admonished as she grabbed the stool from her tulle-covered vanity. "Sit there." She pointed at the bench. "I'm going to do your hair and makeup."

After she finished working her magic, she stepped back to admire her creation. At best, I usually gave the makeup process a lick and a promise. A little powder, a swipe of mascara and a dab of lipstick, and I called it good. Not tonight.

I could subdue her, I thought as I sat in a fragrant cloud of Aqua Net and Estée Lauder awaiting the verdict. Bunny walked around me humming some inane tune.

"You are gorgeous! Absolutely fan-tab-u-lous. I've outdone myself this time." She broke into an immense smile and turned me around to check my appearance in her cheval mirror.

"Holy cow! I've got boobs." Did I ever! They were falling out of the top of the dress for God and everyone to see. As short as the skirt was, it looked like my legs went on forever.

The problem was that Bunny's little dress barely covered the essentials. I didn't know whether to pull it up or pull it down. As for the rest of it, Bunny was right. I was gorgeous. Could I possibly be a swan?

"Your parents would have a cow if they could see you. You are one bitchin' chick!" Bunny exclaimed.

She was right. Mama and Daddy would stroke out if they set eyes on me. I loved them dearly, really I did, but being a good girl was tiresome sometimes. I sympathized wholeheartedly with all the preachers' kids I knew. Living in a fishbowl was hell.

"It shouldn't take long for your transformation to hit the grapevine." Bunny giggled, then went into her Captain Bligh impersonation. "Don't touch a hair on your head. I'll get dressed and we'll get rolling."

When Bunny was right, she was right. Being a foxy mama was quite a high. What was Charlie going to say? And why did I care? Could it be because I was obsessed with someone I couldn't have?

Conversation ceased when we walked into the party. Guys I'd known since kindergarten stared at me, their mouths hanging open. Pretty cool, huh?

I was reveling in my new state of glamour when Charlie showed up.

"Hey, Sunshine. You're looking mighty good," he said, putting his arm around Bunny's waist. It wasn't a bad reaction, but it wasn't especially good, either. What did I think he was going to do, ditch Bunny and declare his undying love for me?

Get real.

I'd driven to the party with Bunny, so I hoped I wouldn't have to hitch a ride home. That was getting old. And seeing her with Charlie was even more depressing.

"Jazzy, I'm glad you came. I've been waiting for you." Petey grabbed my hand and pulled me across the room. He was the only guy who was immune to my new attractions. The whole sexy thing was fun, but normalcy was good, too.

"I've got someone I want you to meet. My cousin is here from Dallas. I told you about him, remember?" Petey kept tugging on my hand. I could have easily pulled him to a halt, but everyone was staring. So I went into docile mode and followed him.

Petey halted in front of the most gorgeous guy I'd ever clapped eyes on. This person was related to *Petey*—band-geek Petey?

The hunk had dark hair and ice-blue eyes. Oh, wow, was that a deadly combo.

"Jazzy, this is my cousin Clint Whitworth. Clint's going to be a sophomore at Southern Methodist."

Only Petey would call SMU Southern Methodist.

"Clint, this is my friend Jazzy." Petey was grinning as if he'd just won a jackpot. "Her name is really Jasmine but we all call her Jazzy," he explained, and continued to stare at us as if he was expecting something exciting to happen.

"Miss Jasmine, you are beautiful," the

Adonis said, taking my hand and kissing my palm.

I was almost afraid I'd faint dead away. I didn't know whether the dizziness came from lust or the waist-cincher that was restricting my blood flow.

"Let's find a quiet place to get to know each other." Clint guided me through the crowd to the pool, where we sat in lounge chairs and talked. We interrupted our conversation only to raid the buffet and dangle our feet in the water. It seemed we had everything in common. We enjoyed the same music, books, school subjects, and we even saw eye to eye on politics.

Clint told me he'd just finished his freshman year and that he planned to go to law school. When I explained I wanted to be an architect, he didn't laugh. I even confided that I'd been drawing houses since I was in elementary school. Very few people were privy to the information that I got off on the idea of designing homes.

Although it was the 1970s, male chauvinism was alive and well in Meadow Lake, and women were not encouraged to step outside the few professions deemed *acceptable*. Even the school counselors said I should reconsider my choice. What did they know?

Clint, however, said he thought it was a great idea. And that alone sent him to the top of my favorite-people list.

This newfound comradeship was very cool. It felt like I'd known him forever. Petey grinned like a kid in a candy store every time he looked at us. Discretion wasn't exactly his middle name.

"Cousin Petey is a matchmaker," Clint said. "He's been trying to introduce us for over a year. He claims we're made for each other."

"Really?" Sounds lame, I know, but what else could I say to his comment?

"Yeah, imagine that."

What did *that* mean?

I glanced around and didn't see either Charlie or Bunny. Darn it! "This has been great, it really has, but it looks like Bunny went off with Charlie so I need to hit up someone for a ride home." I wasn't hinting for him to take me home, honestly I wasn't. Uh-uh.

"I'll take you whenever you're ready to go."

I hated to admit my social shortcomings to a college guy, especially one with Paul Newman eyes. "Midnight is my curfew," I finally admitted, although it took a few false starts for me to get it out.

"Oh." Although he looked a bit non-plussed, he recovered quickly. "I'll tell Petey we're going."

And that's how we ended up parked out by the river in his new Datsun 240Z.

"Petey showed me this place. I thought since we had half an hour to kill, we could talk."

If that was his euphemism for necking, it seemed like a great idea to me. I couldn't think of anything I'd like better than to get into a good lip-lock with him. Obviously Charlie would be my first preference, but that wasn't going to happen. Not now, not ever.

"Sure," I said.

So there we were, sitting in the moonlight

with the cicadas creating their own brand of soft music. It was romance at its best—if you discounted the damned stick shift between us. I leaned my head back against the soft leather seat and fantasized about what would happen next.

Guess what? Nothing happened, because Clint kept yakking on and on about freshman English.

Freshman English! I was about to melt into a puddle of hormonal angst and he was analyzing Hemingway?

Enough was enough. If he wasn't going to make the first move I'd have to take matters into my own hands.

Ignoring everything ladylike that Mama had tried to drill into my head, I launched myself at him.

It took about half a second to realize I'd made a terrible mistake.

As a virgin I wasn't familiar with erotic sounds; however, even I knew that a yelp wasn't a harbinger of lust.

After he disentangled our body parts, he planted a kiss on my forehead. Nope, that definitely wasn't lust.

"Um, Jaz, um, there's something I need to tell you."

If it was possible to die from embarrassment, I was about to expire on the spot. By that time I had managed to wiggle back into my seat. Something was drastically wrong.

"What?"

He sighed as if the weight of the world was on his shoulders. "I'm sorry. I should've told you sooner."

Oh, my God, he thought I was too skinny, or maybe he thought I was butt-ugly. Or worse, I had a stray piece of spinach in my teeth.

"Told me what?" I managed to squeak.

"I, uh…" He paused. "Crap, this is hard."

This time I didn't interrupt him.

"I have a good friend who's a guy."

So what? "Some of my best friends are guys."

He stared at me in amazement and then lapsed into a heartfelt chuckle. "Sometimes I forget about life in a small town." He gave me one of those looks that said *hey, dummy, I'm saying something important here.* "He's a *really* good friend."

Oh. My. God! If they gave out stupidity awards I'd have a blue ribbon. "You mean you're…" Somehow I couldn't finish the sentence, especially considering the fact that I'd almost ravished him.

"Yeah, I am." He leaned over the console and looked me in the eye. "I've really enjoyed being with you tonight. I hope we can be friends."

"Sure, I'd love to be your friend." He was smart, he was funny, he was a great conversationalist—and unfortunately, this major dreamboat wasn't interested in girls.

If that didn't beat all!

Chapter 4

"Jazzy, is he as scrumptious as I heard?" Misty plopped down on the dock where I was sunbathing. "Can you believe that nerdy Petey has a cousin who looks like a movie star?"

She scooted to the edge of the dock and put her feet in the water. "And I was having dinner with my *parents!* Are you going to see him again and does he have any friends?"

Oh, yeah, he had friends. But I wasn't planning to share that even with *my* good friend. Whether he told anyone or not was his business.

I glanced up from painting my toenails and gave a heartfelt sigh. "He was, uh—he was nice." I shook my head, pondering the abominable luck I had with boys. That led me straight back to Charlie and my unrequited love. I hated that term. It sounded like something out of a Jane Austen novel.

Oh, Mr. Darcy, my love for you is unrequited.

"So, are you going to see him again? Is he coming back anytime soon?"

"Get a grip, Misty," I snapped. Uh-oh, losing my cool was a big mistake, especially with our budding attorney. I was never grumpy, not even when it was that time of the month. Now Misty would definitely know something was up.

"What?" She had that crafty look I hated so much.

"Nothing."

"Don't you *nothin'* me, girlie. You're keeping a secret and I want to know what it is."

"Hey, y'all." Those dulcet tones came from Bunny.

I was saved by my bleached-blonde friend. She strutted down to the dock in the shortest, tightest pair of cutoffs I'd ever seen. "Aren't those uncomfortable?" I had to ask.

"Nope." She slipped her sandals off and sat down on the dock. "Let's go riding."

Cruising was our favorite hobby. Of course, in Meadow Lake, cruising was one of the few things a kid could do for entertainment.

"Sounds good to me," Misty said. "I don't have to be home for dinner until seven."

"And I don't have to go to work until tomorrow." In my summer gig as a lifeguard, I worked a couple of days a week. It was a hard job—yeah, right—but someone had to do it.

"Where's Mary Alice?" Bunny asked.

"Her dad's holding a revival meeting. She told me they're going down to the river to do some baptizing," Misty answered.

Bunny laughed. "I guess riding around with us is out, huh?"

"Yep." Mary Alice missed quite a few things the rest of us called fun.

Even though it was hotter than hell, we had the convertible top down. We were willing to sacrifice anything in the name of being "cool," and believe it or not, that included scorched thighs.

We circled the Pink Pig several times. At three o'clock in the afternoon the pickings were slim.

"I have an idea," Bunny said.

It wasn't so much what she said as how she said it. The way my skin prickled, I knew we were heading for a mess of trouble. But before my good sense could issue a stern warning, Misty piped up.

"What?" she asked.

Bunny wore her "we're gonna be oh, so grounded if anyone catches us" grin.

"We're going skinny-dipping in the park."

"No!" I shouted, almost causing her to run into a stop sign.

"Why not?" Bunny put on her affronted act.

"Because my daddy's the police chief and if we get caught I'll be a hundred and ten years old before I'm allowed to leave the house again."

"Don't worry about it. I have everything under control." She turned the car toward the park.

Misty didn't say a word. She was probably wondering whether she could survive jumping from a moving vehicle, because if that girl got nabbed with her drawers down in a public place, her parents would hustle her off to a boarding school that would make Oliver Twist's look plush.

Our friend batted away our objections as if they were pesky gnats. So off to the river we went, the three of us like lemmings to the sea.

The park had a long winding roadway between the golf course and the water. River Road was popular with the high-school crowd for a couple of reasons—most of which made my daddy cranky. The Indy 500 wannabes used it to hone their racing skills, and the "parkers" favored the secluded areas to do whatever it was lovers did, not that I was an expert on *that,* being a virgin and all.

For this particular exploit we had to have privacy. My bare butt was not appropriate viewing material.

Bunny pulled into the small lot adjacent to a picnic area at the end of the drive. At that time of day, in that heat, the chances of running into a family were pretty slight. Anyone with a lick of sense was inside enjoying the air-conditioning.

"You guys coming? You'll love it."

Bunny was out of the car and halfway down the hill before Misty and I could decide what to do. Darn it, she started flapping her arms up and down making clucking noises. Who could ignore a challenge like that?

"I hate being manipulated," I muttered. And that's what my friend was doing, in spades.

"Me, too," Misty admitted. "But I can't seem to resist."

"Yeah," I said as I unfolded my long legs from the backseat of the very small car. Please God, don't let one of Daddy's patrolmen do the park loop and check on Bunny's car.

* * *

Okay, Bunny was right. Shucking your clothes and skinny-dipping was decadence at its best. It was a cross between being naughty and feeling liberated.

"This is nice. But I'm still worried about snakes," I said as I rolled over to float on my back. The only way a cottonmouth water moccasin could bite you was to latch on to a small appendage, and I had two small appendages that I did *not* want bitten, and we weren't talking about fingers.

I'd always thought floating was as close as you could get to being back in the womb. It was very quiet and it gave you a serene sense of weightlessness.

"Who's that?" Misty hissed.

I felt my tranquility take a nosedive. I jackknifed in the water just in time to see my so-called friends swimming as fast as they could toward the other side of the river.

"Hey, you!" It was a male voice. An *irritated* male voice.

Oh, great! It was none other than Eddie Troyer, Daddy's newest patrolman.

Fortunately, I was far enough out in the

water that he probably didn't recognize me. Unfortunately, he was standing next to our pile of clothes.

Darn it all!

When I trained as a lifeguard I did a lot of underwater swimming. With Patrolman Troyer hot on my tail, I was certainly glad I'd learned how to hold my breath for an extended period of time.

"What are we going to do?" Bunny asked.

The three of us were crouching in the bushes as we watched the cop prowl up and down the opposite bank.

"Oh, God," I moaned. "He probably thinks we've drowned and he's gonna call my daddy. They'll bring a boat out and drag the river. We *have* to let them know we're not dead."

"No," Misty whined.

"Wait, wait, wait." Bunny seemed to be the only one whose brain was still working.

"He has to go back to his car to report this, right?"

"Yeah." I could almost see where she was going with this.

"When he climbs back up the hill, we race across, grab our clothes and hide in the bushes downstream."

"That might work." And if it didn't, the rookie was going to get an up-close-and-personal preview of my ass. But as repugnant as that seemed, I didn't have a better idea.

"I'm in."

"Me, too," Misty reluctantly agreed.

She didn't sound all that sure, but neither was I, so we were even.

The minute Eddie turned his back and trudged up the hill, we were in the water swimming like we'd jumped into a pool of piranhas.

Bunny was the first out of the water, first to grab her shorts and first to disappear into the bushes. I was right behind her. Panic and adrenaline made me very fast.

"What are we going to do about your car?" The vehicle question was something that had occurred to me the minute my brain started working. How could we explain the car? We certainly couldn't drive past Patrolman Troyer, waving blithely on our way out.

We'd found sanctuary behind some wild grapevines. I had my underwear on, Bunny was already in her shorts and halter top, and all Misty could manage to do was sit there and moan.

"Not to worry. I have an idea," Bunny announced—not for the first time.

It was a good thing she did; I was considering turning myself in and facing the consequences.

"You guys stay here while I sneak over to the parking lot," Bunny instructed. "I'll take that little cart path behind the eighteenth hole. As soon as he wanders off, I'll hop in the car and sneak away. Then he won't see me leave—and if he does, at least you guys won't get caught."

"So what do we do?" Misty asked.

"You guys walk back to the clubhouse and call someone dependable to come and get you. If anyone asks why my car was at the park, I'll play dumb."

"That might work." It sounded half-baked to me but at least it was a plan. And that surpassed anything I could suggest.

"It'll work. We just have to stick together.

Skinny-dipping, are you kidding? We're nice girls. That's our story. Deal?" Bunny put out her hand.

"Deal." I slapped my palm on top of hers. This was one of the benefits of sisterhood. All for one, and one for all.

"Do you think Bunny got away?" Misty whispered as we approached the clubhouse.

I'd lost my shoes somewhere, and even worse, Misty's bra had vanished. Add that to the fact her T-shirt was wet, and we had a big problem.

"Before we go inside you need to pull your shirt out and fan yourself. Maybe it'll dry a little."

"Aargh!" Misty apparently hadn't noticed the way the cotton was molded to her chest. "I can't go in there, not like this." She made wild waving motions with her hands.

"I agree. You hunker down over there in the lawn chair. I'll see if they'll let me use their phone."

"Who are you going to call?"

That didn't take much thought. I planned

to call my best buddy. "Charlie will get us. He's the only person I really trust."

Wasn't that annoying? The one person I felt I could turn to in a crisis was my good friend's boyfriend.

"What have you girls gotten yourselves into now?" Charlie barely managed to control his chuckles when he asked the question.

All I'd had to tell him was that we needed a ride and he was on his way to retrieve us. No questions, no comments, just a "hang on, I'll be there in a few minutes." Thank goodness!

Misty's wild red curls had dried into a mess that resembled a Bozo the Clown wig, and heaven knows what I looked like. The term "raccoon eyes" came to mind.

"Is this gonna burn up the grapevine?" he asked.

Misty and I answered simultaneously. Her answer was an emphatic no. I was a bit more circumspect with my "I hope not. God, I hope not."

Our answers brought another round of laughter from our chauffeur.

"Here we are." He pulled up behind Misty's house. "Are you okay?"

"Yep. Jaz, I'll call you. Thanks, Charlie," she said before she dashed toward her back door.

Charlie turned to me, a serious expression on his face. "Is your daddy gonna meet us with one of those bad-cop looks?"

"Not if we're lucky," I said with fervor.

"Lord, you're enough to give a guy gray hair." He punctuated his assertion by rubbing the top of my head.

"Do you remember the time in the fourth grade when Hooter Thompson knocked me off the jungle gym and you gave him a black eye?" I'd wanted to ask that question for years. It was the defining moment, the moment I knew for certain that I was head over heels in love with Charlie, and my feelings hadn't changed much in the intervening time.

He glanced at me and laughed. He was no doubt wondering why I'd brought up an event that occurred years before. "I remember. I was grounded for a week when the principal called my dad. Why are you asking?"

"No reason."

Charlie hesitated, looking as if he was about to press the issue and then decided against it. "Okay," he said before he started the car.

On the drive to my house, our conversation was strangely stilted. I was contemplating how he was always there for me and how much I loved being around him. He was probably thinking I was a major-league nitwit.

Charlie parked beside our guesthouse. "Let's stroll down to the dock so you can tell me what happened. If I'm about to have another Hooter Thompson experience, I'd like to be prepared."

He was out of the car and around to the passenger side before I could get my butt in gear.

"Come on, Sunshine. You've got some 'splaining to do." He put his arm around me and for a brief moment I imagined what it would be like if we were a couple.

That would be my idea of heaven; too bad Charlie didn't feel the same way.

A couple of days later, I was in the middle of one of my favorite fantasies when the star attraction pulled his boat up to the dock.

"Hey, Sunshine, you want to take a spin?"

Of course I did. I'd go to the moon with this guy.

I was halfway in the boat before I bothered to answer. "Sure. Where are we off to?"

He reached into the cooler and brought out an icy Coke. "I'm starving so I thought we'd head down to Slim Jim's for a burger."

"Good." Slim's had the best French fries north of the Rio Grande. It was the best of all possible worlds; I could enjoy something fattening and also spend a couple of hours with Charlie.

"Where's Bunny?" Why did I have to ask that?

"I don't know. I have a feeling there's something going on, but she's not talking to me about it."

"Really?"

"Yeah, really." He paused, then grinned. "I guess you could say things are pretty dicey with us right now."

text of the "look." The pretend that getting it, I guess. You often see fathers do this thing with their kids.

Chapter 5

Our gang managed to dodge the bullet—sort of. Daddy kept giving me the "look." I knew he knew what we'd been up to; fortunately he couldn't prove it.

Too bad! This was my last opportunity to be a carefree kid and I intended to take advantage of every minute. Yeah, I realized we were being childish, but our tiny bit of hell-raising was our version of asserting our independence.

Summer in Meadow Lake had always had a magical quality—it was sun and fun at its best. And July was truly our summer, a time and place that could never be replicated.

It'd been almost two weeks since our skinny-dipping escapade. I cringed at the thought of what would've happened if the patrolman had caught us butt naked. Darn it, I was *not* about to let Bunny talk me into another debacle. And if I believed that, I was delusional. She was charismatic, mischievous and irresistible to mere mortals.

That's how she managed to snag me for our next escapade. I protested, a little, but it was to no avail. We were heading off to toilet-paper Mr. Hargrove's house, and that antic was guaranteed to land us in a pile of trouble. Not only was he our high-school principal, he was also one of the grumpiest guys in town.

"I certainly hope you bought that stuff at different stores," I whispered as I jumped into Bunny's car. The backseat was filled with rolls of toilet paper.

"Even better, I raided the janitor's closet at Daddy's factory. They'll never be able to trace it to us," she assured me as we rolled quietly down the road. Our covert mission required maximum darkness—read the middle of the night—so we all had to sneak out. I felt like a cat burglar in reverse as I crept out of my house and met Bunny down the road.

I was afraid Mary Alice would chicken out, but there she was, standing on the corner with Misty.

"Good grief," Misty exclaimed, batting the toilet paper out of the way. "Where did you get this junk?"

"I liberated it."

"You *stole* it," Mary Alice squeaked.

"No, you ninny. I'll eventually inherit Daddy's business, so in essence I own everything in that building. Toilet paper and all."

Even I realized *that* was a bit of a stretch. But who was I to criticize? I was in the process of giving Daddy gray hair. Thank goodness Bucky was working as a camp counselor. Brother dearest was the biggest tattletale in the world, and Daddy really didn't need to hear about this stunt.

We cruised past the Hargroves' house several times before we came up with a definitive game plan. We didn't have a ladder—which was probably just as well—so we'd have to make do with papering the bushes.

Total silence was a necessity for successfully completing our mission, and pulling that off would require a miracle. When Mary Alice got in a bind she turned into a giggle box. That wasn't good when you were committing a misdemeanor. Misdemeanor or felony, it wouldn't make a whit of difference to Daddy—breaking the law was breaking the law.

The alley was dark, the town was silent, and other than the odd insomniac and the night clerk at the 7-Eleven, we were the only people up and out. Mary Alice gave another maniacal giggle, managing to wake a dog in the process.

"Stop that," Bunny hissed as she crept into our potential victim's yard. "I have an idea. We can do this tree." She indicated a small mimosa. "Jazzy, since you're so tall, Misty can get on your shoulders and she can throw the toilet paper at least halfway up the tree."

That stopped me in my tracks. "What's this 'we,' kemo sabe? Looks to me like Misty and I will be doing all the work."

Bunny waved her hand in the air. Sometimes that girl really annoyed me.

"Come on, let's do it." Misty dragged me through the hedge and headed straight to our target—a poor, innocent tree.

"Kneel down and I'll get on. Then you can stand up," she instructed me.

"Sure, I bench-press a hundred and ten pounds all the time!"

"Come on, don't be a spoilsport," Bunny said. "I'm too short to do this and so is Mary Alice. We have to finish up and get out of here." She had a roll of toilet paper in each hand.

It was nice of her to remind me I was the only Amazon in a bevy of petites. Uh-huh!

I got down on my knees and allowed Misty to straddle my shoulders. The tricky part would be getting up.

"Hey, you guys, give me a hand," I hissed to my coconspirators.

We were making more noise than a Ringling Brothers circus. I was positive someone had already called the cops, so when Misty fell off my shoulders and we landed in a heap of arms and legs, I knew we were busted. It didn't come as a surprise when the front porch light went on.

"Beat feet," Bunny yelled, dropping the incriminating paper.

Running sounded like one of the best ideas I'd ever heard; too bad Misty was sprawled across me.

"Get up," I demanded. Then I pushed her off and scrambled toward the hedge. Yay for adrenaline and the flight response! I was well hidden in the leafy foliage before my compatriots made it halfway to safety.

By the time we tumbled into Bunny's car, every dog in the neighborhood was barking. The Bennett family must've had some larcenous genes lurking in the background. The way she pulled her car out of the alley, sans lights, was pure genius.

"I about busted a gut." Mary Alice lapsed into a fit of giggles. "I can't believe we did that."

Neither could I. Had I totally taken leave of my senses? Oh right, this was the Goody-

Two-Shoes club's summer of mischief—innocent, of course. And if I could talk Daddy into buying *that* one, I was shoo-in for an Academy Award.

"Where are we going?" Misty asked. She'd obviously recovered her sense of speech. From the moment I pushed her away, until we were well out of the danger zone, moaning had been her only form of communication.

"We're going to the truck stop," Bunny answered, whizzing down Main Street.

The only place in town that was open twenty-four hours a day was the truck-stop restaurant on the interstate.

"I'm hungry for some pecan waffles," the princess of our misadventure informed us before she launched into a boisterous sing-along with Carole King.

"Running from the law makes you hungry, huh?" I asked. My pesky sarcasm reared its ugly head again. I was beginning to doubt our friendship, and that made me sad.

"Yes, ma'am," she said, gracing me with

the dimples that had turned boys all over the county into slobbering idiots.

Bunny was drowning her waffles with syrup. "Are you over your snit?" Her question was directed at me.

"Beg your pardon?" I asked, emphasizing the question with my famous arched eyebrow. Bucky taught me that trick, and I had to admit it made an effective statement.

"So, how does Charlie feel about you going back East to school?" Although Mary Alice, the inveterate peacemaker, was attempting to head off a spat, her choice of questions left a lot to be desired.

"Charlie has nothing to do with where I go to school. I haven't discussed it with him. And it's really none of his business." Bunny punctuated her assertion with a hair flip.

Sometimes that girl was a real bitch. As I watched her, I tried to remember why we were friends. To be totally honest, it was one of those situations where you intellectually acknowledge a person's faults, but for some reason you choose to ignore her shortcomings.

But when it came to her cavalier attitude toward Charlie, she pushed all my buttons. In all probability it was a good thing we were about to scatter to the four winds.

College would be a new beginning for all of us, and I wasn't sure our friendships would survive.

Chapter 6

I think I mentioned I was employed—sort of. That is, if you called sitting by a pool sipping Tab and watching kids play Marco Polo a job. At any rate, every other afternoon and on Saturday mornings, I was a lifeguard at the Meadow Lake Resort where Charlie and Colton gave ski lessons to the debutantes from Houston whose parents owned summer mansions. I referred to those airheads as Bimbos in Bikinis—not that I was jealous of their bosoms or anything.

The days I worked were high on my "look

forward to" list, because I could hang out with Charlie. Every so often Colton would join us. Although they were twins, they were physically as different as night and day. Charlie had the looks of a blond surfer boy while Colton resembled a young Clint Eastwood.

They were both handsome guys, but there was something about Charlie I found irresistible. What's it about sexual chemistry? People through the millennia have asked that question and the answer's always eluded them.

So I continued to pal around with Charlie. We'd talk for hours. At times it felt like we were on a date. On other occasions, it seemed more like a therapy session, especially when he lapsed into a discussion of Bunny.

There was obviously more than a little trouble in paradise; in other words, they were fighting like cats and dogs. I wasn't sure how I felt about that. I wasn't surprised, but I really didn't want Bunny to be hurt. And more importantly, I didn't want *Charlie* hurt.

But Charlie and Bunny's relationship had nothing to do with the day my world went to hell. It started out innocently. I was doing a Saturday-morning shift at the pool. Charlie had some private ski students and Bunny was in San Antonio with her parents.

"Hey, Sunshine." Charlie strolled over to my lifeguard stand. My heart did its usual flip-flop. Darn it, I wished it would stop doing that.

"Would you do me a favor?"

Anything, especially if it involved lots of kissing. That thought deserved a mental slap. "Sure. What do you need?"

"I have a private client coming up from Houston for a lesson this afternoon and Colton's busy so I'd like you to drive the boat." Charlie and his brother made money team-teaching water-ski lessons. One of the twins would drive and the other one would get in the water to assist the student.

"You might remember the guy. His parents own a house out on the island. In fact, I think you dated him a couple of times."

"Are you talking about Stuart Redding?"

"Yeah."

Boy, did I remember that jerk! "I had one date with him." And a team of wild horses couldn't have forced me back into a car with that pervert. He was one of those rich kids who thought a country bumpkin would be an easy lay. One quick jab, and that notion was dispelled!

"He's not very nice."

"What did he do?" Charlie was about to segue into his white-knight routine. No telling how he'd react if I told him about my Stuart encounter.

"Oh, nothing much."

"Are you positive?"

"Yeah. What time do you want me?" I'd been driving a ski boat since before I had a vehicle license, so this would be a no-brainer—plus Stuart was afraid of me.

"Let's say three o'clock."

"Okay."

Later, as I looked back on our conversation, it struck me as ironic that a simple little request could have such a profound impact on my life. My shift was over and I was sipping a Coke when a flashy new Corvette roared up and screeched to a stop. The driver was Stuart "I'm nothing but trouble" Redding.

We'd been on the water almost an hour and Stuart still hadn't managed to get up on the skis. It usually took a six-year-old kid about three tries before he was up and away. I wasn't positive, but I suspected Stuart was a pothead and that affected his coordination.

I'd made the boat stop and start about two dozen times and the guy still couldn't do it. Billy Tom, who happened to be our spotter, and I were placing bets on how soon Stuart would give up.

I felt terrible for Charlie. He'd been in the water so long he probably looked like a California raisin. And that wasn't the worst of it. Even over the rumble of the motor I could hear Stuart cursing. From the snippets I overheard, I knew he'd disparaged Charlie's teaching methods, my driving, the river, the weather and God only knows what else. Yep, he was something, all right.

"Charlie's swimming back to the boat," Billy Tom said.

I cut the engine so Charlie could hoist himself safely onto the rear platform. He heaved his skis aboard and sat there for a few minutes with his head in his hands. Then he grinned at me, brightening my day.

"Hey, Sunshine. You up for one last try?"

"Sure." If he'd asked me to jump off the bridge I would've done it. I would've run with scissors if he'd suggested it.

"I suspect he's a lost cause, but I'm gonna try one more thing. If I get him up, give it enough gas to keep him in an upright position, okay? Go down the river where it's not quite so crowded. I'm leaving my skis here, so after he goes down help him into the boat and come back to get me. I don't think he'll stay up very long. Is that okay?"

"Uh-huh."

Charlie jumped back in the water and paddled over to his student in preparation for another try. When he gave the thumbs-up, I hit the gas and much to my surprise whatever Charlie did worked.

"He's up," Billy yelled.

"Thank goodness," I muttered. The whole thing was getting old.

"Give it more gas. He's a pretty big guy," Billy said. "I want to keep him up as long as possible."

"I do, too." I made a wide, gentle arc into the river. Our passenger did *not* need to get fancy. Experienced skiers preferred the smooth water outside the wake. Novices, on the other hand, were safer within the confines of the boat wave.

"How's he doing?" I shouted to be heard over the roar of the engine.

"Fine," Billy said, and then amended his assessment. "Uh-oh. He's out in the smooth water. I wonder how he managed that?"

Yeah, how did he do it? It took some measure of control to jump the slight swell created by the boat, and control wasn't his forte.

I decided the derelict Two Mile Bridge would be a great turning-around place. We could go under the bridge and I'd slow down to allow our student to sink into the water. Then we'd retrieve him and this fiasco would be over.

Too bad it didn't happen that way. Not even close.

"Stop, stop, stop!" Billy screamed. "Stop! Oh, God. Oh, God. Oh, God!"

It was the desperation of his last "Oh, God" that prompted me to jerk back on the throttle, stalling the engine.

"What?" I launched myself from the driver's seat and ran to the rear of the boat.

I looked toward where our student should've been, but there was no one in sight. The only thing I could see was the yellow nylon ski rope stretched out behind us.

"He hit the bridge pillar." Billy put his hands on his head and rocked back and forth. "Oh, my God! Shit! He hit the bridge!"

"He did what?" I wanted to smack Billy. "What? What did he do?" Surely Billy was wrong.

"He hit the bridge," Billy Tom moaned. "He smacked into the concrete!"

My heart flapped around like a landed bass, but I somehow maintained enough awareness to know we had to do something.

"Pull in the rope, Billy! Right now!" My tone of voice must have penetrated his building panic, because he did as I instructed.

I turned the boat around and slowly motored back to the bridge. Please, God, please, God, please, please, please—Billy had to be wrong.

"There he is." Billy spotted Stuart's orange life vest. "Damn! Damn! Damn! Look at his neck."

One glance at the unnatural angle of his head and I about lost it. He had to be dead. With all that blood in the water, he had to be dead.

Dead!

I motored up next to the body and Billy was in the water almost before I cut the engine. He was now issuing orders. I, on the other hand, was but an inch from pure terror.

"I'm going to take him to shore," Billy called. He had Stuart in a rescue hold and was swimming to the riverbank.

"Drive over to that dock and see if someone's home. We have to call the cops," he shouted.

I wanted my daddy. He could make everything better, I told myself. But could he really?

I barely had the boat stopped before I was out of it and sprinting up the hill, praying that someone would be home.

"Help us," I screeched, beating on the door. My guardian angel must've been working overtime. Thank you, God!

Mrs. Thompson was a tiny woman with steel-gray hair. "Take a deep breath and put your head between your legs," she told me.

After she was sure I wasn't going to pass out, she asked, "What's the problem?"

Somehow between sobs, I managed to spit out my story. By that time, Mr. Thompson had joined us. He was the one who called for the rescue units.

Mrs. Thompson was a retired nurse and she ran with me to where Billy Tom had laid Stuart on the grass. Regrettably there was no need for medical assistance. She confirmed my worst suspicion; Stuart was not returning to his good life in the Corvette lane.

"Someone has to go downriver to get Charlie." My teeth were chattering like castanets, making it hard to get the words out.

"Charlie?" Mr. Thompson asked.

"Yeah, he was teaching Stuart to ski and he dropped off in the water over that way." I nodded toward Charlie's location.

Looking back on it, I think I scared Mr. Thompson half to death. The way he jumped into his boat and sped off, he must've thought he was about to find another dead body.

It seemed like an eternity, although it was probably just a matter of minutes before he returned with Charlie.

"Oh, Charlie." That was all I could say before I broke into tears.

"It's okay. I promise, it'll be okay." He sank down on the grass where I was huddled in one of Mrs. Thompson's blankets.

Damn, I was cold.

"Listen to me," Charlie commanded. "It wasn't your fault."

He enveloped me in an embrace. He was warm. He was safe. And my world had just imploded.

"Sweetheart, are you all right?" Much to my surprise, Daddy was sitting on the ground next to me. Where had he come from?

I looked up and was astonished to see a fleet of fire and police vehicles.

"I'm taking you home." Daddy pulled me to my feet and propelled me in the direction of his cruiser. "Come on, boys, I'll drive you home, too. Tomorrow will be plenty of time to talk about what happened."

Chapter 7

It had been two days since the accident, but every time I closed my eyes there it was, running again and again like a bad movie. Stuart's eyes were open and sightless, and his ear almost touched his shoulder. Would I ever be able to get that sight out of my mind?

All my life I'd been the queen of guilt—I felt guilty, or perhaps a better word was *responsible*—about situations that were way beyond my control. For instance, I felt horribly guilty when Mary Alice didn't have a date for the junior prom and I did.

He happened to be a total dork, but he was still a date.

Then there was the case of the taco stand that went out of business. Somehow I convinced myself that if I'd stopped there more often, the guy might still be around. In general, the guilt was annoying but bearable. This fiasco had taken it to a new plane.

"I got some of your favorite sweet rolls at the Dixie Delite." Mama was standing in my bedroom door holding a bakery box. She was doing her best to cheer me up. In fact, my parents were spoiling me rotten. On one level, it was nice. On another, it was making me crazy. Instinctively, I realized I had to get out of bed and face the situation. However, knowing and doing were two entirely different things.

"Thanks, Mom. I'm going to take a shower. I'll be down in a few minutes."

I could tell by the smile on her face, she was delighted that I was slowly, but surely, coming back to life. My mood was actually rather strange. Sometimes I felt perfectly fine and then it would hit me like a brick.

I was to blame for a person's death. That's when I'd plunge into depression.

I trudged to the shower. Even when things got really bad, there was something rejuvenating about an orgy of hot water.

Before I made it down the stairs, I heard voices in the kitchen. Could that be Charlie? I hadn't seen him since the day Daddy took him home to help explain the situation to his parents. He had to be feeling as bad as I did. So why hadn't I called him?

Although Daddy said the official coroner's decision was an accidental death, and there wouldn't be an inquest, I was sure the Morrisons were worried silly. Their boat and their son were involved.

However, he hadn't been driving the boat. I had.

"Hi, Charlie." He was sitting at the table with my mother, munching on a sweet roll.

"Hey, Sunshine. You're looking better," he replied between bites.

That exaggeration required a very unladylike snort. "Better than what?" I was wearing my rattiest shorts, my hair was wet and pulled up into a ponytail, and I didn't have on a dab of makeup.

Mama put a glass of milk and a pastry on the table in front of me. The combination of warm cinnamon and sugar jump-started my taste buds. All of a sudden, I was ravenous.

By the time I'd plowed through three Dixie Delite specials, I was stuffed.

"I see your appetite's returned," Charlie teased. "Why don't you ride down to the dam with me?"

"Okay."

"Mrs. Boudreaux, we'll be back in a little bit."

Mama had always been impressed with Charlie's manners. The guy could charm the birds out of the trees, and regardless of their age, people of the female persuasion were particularly susceptible to his charisma.

"That's fine," Mama said. She likely would've agreed to anything that got me out of the house.

"How are you feeling, really?" Charlie asked after he parked in a gravel spot near the river.

For some inexplicable reason he entwined his fingers with mine.

"I guess I'm okay. How are *you* doing?"

He shrugged. "I feel like crap. He was my responsibility. I knew he couldn't ski, and I also knew he was the kind of guy who'd take dangerous chances. I should've told him to get lost, but I didn't."

Charlie looked so sad I reached out to touch his cheek. "Neither one of us is to blame. You didn't have any idea he'd act that stupid. And I was being careful, I know I was. That's what my brain says, anyway. My heart tells me something different."

He nodded. "That's why I wanted to talk to you. Only someone who was there would understand." We stared at each other for a long time before Charlie continued.

"I feel so responsible." I felt a tear trickle down my cheek. "He died. He's not here anymore and that's heartbreaking."

"Sunshine." Charlie traced the path of the tear with his finger. "Please don't cry." He put his arms around me. "It's my fault. I should've told him to go home." He rubbed my back.

"It was an accident," he said. "Honestly it was. I've been worried about you. I didn't see it happen, and later he was covered up with a sheet. I'd never met him, so I didn't have any personal connection with him."

"I didn't really know him, either. The one date we had was a disaster. He kept wanting to put his hands where I didn't want him to, and when he wouldn't take no for an answer I kneed him in the, uh, you know."

"You kneed him?" Charlie asked with a chuckle.

"Guilty."

"Oh, boy," he said with a grimace. "Remind me not to make you mad."

His comment broke the oppressive mood that threatened to overwhelm us. "Come with me," Charlie said.

Once we got out of the car, he pulled me to the base of the dam. I thought we were going down to the water; however, he made a right turn before we got to the concrete.

"This is my secret spot." Charlie gestured at a bower of green hidden by a large willow tree. "I come down here when I need to meditate."

He was wearing a sheepish little-boy expression that made me fall more in love with him than ever.

"The only other person who knows about this place is Colton. But I brought you here because I suspect you need a retreat."

How *did* he know that was exactly what I was craving? And how, in all the years of playing in this meadow, had I missed this heavenly space? I wasn't sure whether it was the lush greenery or the breeze dancing through the trees that made it so extraordinary, but whatever it was, I sensed that I'd been brought here for a reason.

"Would you like to talk?"

That was like asking a lion if he'd be interested in a wildebeest snack. The funny thing was, we didn't talk; we simply relaxed and watched the water.

Charlie was reclining in the grass with his hands behind his head. "Are you ready to go to California?"

That was a good question, and one no one else had bothered to ask.

I grimaced, pondering my many misgivings, my middle-of-the-night fears. "I'm kinda scared. It'll sure be different. Are you and Colton still planning to go to UT?"

"Yeah." He levered himself up on one arm. "There are two of us and money's tight, so we couldn't get very exotic in our choice of schools."

After that, we talked, we laughed, and we shared memories from our childhood. It was an afternoon I'd remember forever, one of those rare and idyllic moments. As we discussed our college futures, I was surprised to discover that Charlie wanted to be a doctor. We'd been friends forever, but I didn't know that. And Charlie was totally enthusiastic about my dream of becoming a world-class architect. His unconditional acceptance was another reason I loved him.

I was hunched over with my chin on my knees when Charlie started playing with my ponytail. As far as I was concerned, he could do that all day.

"You have beautiful hair. It feels like silk." He emphasized his point by gently removing the rubber band and sifting the strands through his fingers.

Oh, definitely, he could do that forever.

"I, um, I think I should tell you that Bunny and I broke up. Other than Colton, you're the first person I've told." He continued to play with my hair.

His fingers tangled in the strands when I jerked around to face him. "You broke up?"

"Yep, we did."

"Why?" And why was I being such a masochist?

"It was a mutual thing. For me, the drama was getting old, and I felt she was using me to thumb her nose at her parents."

I thought so, too, but I wisely kept quiet.

"And as for Bunny, I think she got tired of me. She's always wanted someone sophisticated, and I'm not exactly a Sean Connery type."

Nope, he was better than any James Bond. At least, he was to me.

"I wouldn't be able to do *this* if I still had feelings for Bunny." Charlie put his hand at the nape of my neck and drew me into his arms. I could tell that he wanted to kiss me as much as I wanted to kiss him. And now that he and Bunny weren't dating, I didn't have to feel guilty.

His kiss was soft but demanding. His tongue was moving sensuously back and forth—it was erotic but somehow innocent. The kiss was everything I'd ever imagined, and more.

I briefly wondered whether this was one of those reaffirmation moments in a time of tragedy, and then decided I didn't care.

"Oh, yes," I murmured when I could finally take a breath. My response was enough to encourage him to take the kiss further, to a place I'd never been.

Like any teenager, I'd been out parking, but it had never been anything like this. Perhaps that was because those boys hadn't meant anything to me. Charlie was different. I was almost afraid to admit, even to myself, that I thought of him as my destiny. Maybe that sounds like teenage melodrama, but deep inside it was how I felt.

We lay back in the fragrant grass. It occurred to me that lying in the grass was a good way to get chiggers. But did I care?

Every other cogent or commonsense thought flew out of my mind the minute Charlie unbuttoned my blouse and gently caressed my breasts. Those puppies were A cups at best. This was the moment of reckoning. He didn't seem to mind my lack of assets. Not at all. He kissed them, and stroked them, and generally drove me out of my mind.

So this was what everyone was raving about. In-te-resting. Very interesting…

Things were about to get *more* interesting when we were interrupted by the sound of a car and then a voice.

"Charlie, are you out here?"

"It's Colton," Charlie mumbled. "Crap!" he said with heartfelt fervor. "Let me tie it up for you." He had my halter secured before I could blink an eye.

"Stay here, I'll be right back." Charlie stalked out of our secret place—not his, *ours*—to confront his twin.

Although I could hear their voices, I couldn't understand any of the words. Minutes later a car door slammed, an engine started and Charlie reappeared.

"I'd better take you home." He helped me to my feet and planted a kiss on my forehead. My forehead. Some comment of

Colton's had riled him up. I would gladly have throttled that boy.

"Okay," I murmured reluctantly.

I was innocent and naive, and for sure I was a virgin, but even I could tell when someone was turned on.

This wasn't over—not by a long shot.

Chapter 8

The next week went by in a fog. Mama and Daddy assumed I was sad about the accident. And while that was true, I was also fixated on Charlie. Charlie of all people! In fact, I wasn't simply fantasizing; I was obsessively reviewing our afternoon down by the dam. It was like a delicious movie that played over and over in my mind.

Charlie and Bunny were no longer a couple. How about that? In my private fantasy world, he loved me. Was I being silly? Could we really develop a relationship? I didn't have the answers, but by gosh, I planned to try. The thing that bothered me was that he hadn't called. He had a phone, I had a phone; it wasn't that difficult.

I was enjoying the sounds of summer and swinging in the hammock when Mama came out onto the patio.

"Mary Alice is on the phone. She says it's important."

"Okay." With Mary Alice something important could mean anything from the wrong color of nail polish to a collapse of the stock market. On second thought, she wouldn't have a clue if the economy crashed.

"Hey, M.A. What's happenin'?"

"I got a call from Bunny. She wants to meet us at the Forum Restaurant in Star Gate Mall. I'm getting a bad feeling about this."

The Forum was the most expensive restaurant in the glitziest mall in San Antonio. My budget ran more to burgers at the Pink Pig.

"Don't worry. She probably needs us to help her pick out a dress. You know how melodramatic she can be," I said with a confidence I didn't quite feel—especially since I knew about the breakup. What if she wanted Charlie back?

"I really didn't like the way she sounded." Mary Alice's comment made me nervous. "Like what?"

"Like she'd been crying. I'll call Misty and see if she can come. Bunny specifically said she wants to talk to all of us. Can you drive?"

"Sure, I'll pick you up."

"I hope we can afford this," Mary Alice muttered under her breath as we were led to the table Bunny had reserved.

"My sentiments exactly." The starched white tablecloths were more than a bit disconcerting.

Bunny and I hadn't talked since my afternoon with Charlie. And yes, I had been avoiding her. I didn't know what to say.

The maître d' seated us with a flourish, then informed us that Miss Bennett would be along presently. The ersatz British butler fluffed Mary Alice's napkin before he deposited it in her lap. Did he think we were such hicks that we couldn't figure out what to do with a napkin?

"There she is," Misty said.

Bunny looked horrible, and that was very un-Bunnyish. To be truthful, she looked like she'd lost her best friend. Before she reached the table, she squared her shoulders and plastered on a phony smile. And then, in true Bunny fashion, she sat down and nonchalantly picked up the menu.

"Thanks for meeting me."

I could see tears starting to pool in her eyes, so I grabbed her hand in an effort to comfort her.

"What's wrong? Tell us and maybe we can help make things better," I said. Mary Alice and Misty nodded in agreement.

When the hinted tears became a deluge, all we could do was hang on for dear life.

"I'm pregnant," she hiccupped, then launched into a fresh display of waterworks.

I glanced at my friends. Misty's mouth was hanging open. Mary Alice looked as if she was about to faint. I wanted to rant and rave and scream. As sure as God made little green apples, that baby belonged to Charlie.

"My parents are making me go to Houston to live with my aunt. Then we'll decide what I'm going to do."

As much as I wanted to stick my head in the sand, I had to ask. "Have you told Charlie?"

Bunny was wiping her face with a napkin. "I'm not going to tell him. If I know Charlie, he'll feel it's his problem, and I'm not ready to have that kind of commitment with anyone. Besides, we broke up. So it's none of his business."

"Good Lord," Mary Alice mumbled.

Amen to that! It would take heavenly intervention to straighten out this mess.

"When are you going to Houston?" Misty asked.

"I'm leaving tonight. I'm not even going home, and that's why I wanted you to come here. I don't know when I'll see you again. I want you to promise you won't tell *anyone,* especially Charlie. Promise?"

Mary Alice, Misty and I turned to one another and in unison choked out a reluctant pledge. Then we hugged and cried. The most precious part of our childhood, and our innocence, was irreparably destroyed. Bunny would always bear the scars of love, or lust, or the teenage hormones that had motivated her relationship with Charlie. And we would be forced to keep her secret.

Charlie. I felt so bad for him. On a visceral level I knew he'd be devastated. Bunny and her family had discounted Charlie's rights as the baby's father. Regardless of the fact that Bunny and Charlie didn't love each other, and they no longer had a relationship, the baby was Charlie's and he should have some say in the matter.

I wasn't surprised at the Bennetts' reaction. Bunny was a different story. But who was I to judge? I didn't have to walk in her shoes.

My own were uncomfortable enough.

Chapter 9

It was almost a week before I saw Charlie. I was walking out of the post office when he pulled up in his mom's car.

"Hey, Sunshine. Let's go to the Chocolate Cow."

The Chocolate Cow was the local ice-cream parlor, usually patronized by the blue-haired crew and families with small children. In other words, our chances of encountering anyone we knew would be slim. Was that good or bad?

It took me a second to make up my mind.

"Okay," I said with some measure of fore-boding. What if he grilled me about Bunny?

We rode in silence to the restaurant. What could I say? Not much if I wanted to honor my promise.

Charlie came back from the counter with my hot-fudge sundae. If all else failed, I could rely on chocolate—lots and lots of gooey chocolate.

Always the gentleman, he started off with the usual questions. How was everything going? How were my parents? He did not, however, mention our interlude at the dam. And that didn't bode well for the rest of our conversation.

Then he got down to business. "What do you know about Bunny?"

"Um, I uh, um." Rumors were flying all over town about her sudden disappearance. I had no idea what to say, so I didn't say anything.

He suddenly hit the table so hard the silverware rattled. "I want to know what's going on. I *need* to know."

My heart ached for him. Charlie was frustrated and angry, and who could blame him?

He should have been a major player in this drama, but they'd decided to exclude him. There wasn't anything I could do. I couldn't betray Bunny's confidence.

"I don't know anything."

"Yeah, right," he sneered. "We've been friends all our lives, and I'd bet the pink slip on my car that you're lying."

I didn't bother to deny it as I kept shoveling ice cream into my mouth. Assuming adult responsibility was *definitely* overrated.

Leave it to Charlie to realize when he'd hit a brick wall, at least when it came to dealing with me.

"I'll find out what's going on, don't you doubt it," he announced before stalking out.

Oh, I didn't doubt it, not for a minute. My only consolation was that even after he discovered Bunny's deception, he'd eventually be okay. He was a survivor and survivors always came out on top.

We worked at the same place so it was almost impossible to avoid him, although I'd been giving it the old college try. Charlie was steering clear of me, too. Just being around him felt uncomfortable. I hated that!

Damn Bunny! I thought I'd found my soul mate and somehow she managed to screw it up. Never mind. In three weeks I'd be California bound. I could hold my breath for that long.

Couldn't I?

I'd finished a shift at the pool and was tossing my lifeguard paraphernalia into my beach bag when a familiar voice stopped me in my tracks. It was Colton.

"Charlie heard what's going on with Bunny. I can't believe you let him find out something that important from a busybody at the supermarket. You're supposed to be his friend. Hell, you're supposed to be *my* friend," he said. "This town makes me crazy."

Get in line, buddy, it makes everyone nuts. Why the hell would anyone with half a brain pop that on him, especially while standing in line at the Super Saver?

It took everything I had to meet Colton's eye. I felt horrible about my role in the fiasco, peripheral though it was.

"I am *so* sorry." I touched his arm. "Please tell Charlie that if he ever wants to talk, I'm available." So much for objective detachment.

He shot me a look I couldn't quite interpret. "I'll tell him, but I doubt he'll call you."

Fair enough. It broke my heart, but it certainly seemed like karmic retribution.

Charlie didn't call and he didn't try to contact me. Rumors, however, raged through town like a wildfire. The Age of Aquarius was at its apex, and although an "anything goes" attitude might be popular in California, Meadow Lake, Texas, population 8,631, was a century behind. Let's just say there were some lines you didn't cross, and an out-of-wedlock baby ranked right up there with blasphemy and stealing from parking meters.

To make a really bad situation worse, Charlie and Colton had become social pariahs. For Colton it was guilt by association, but whatever the reason, the Morrison twins were personas non grata.

That made me madder than hell!

A couple of days after my Colton encounter, Misty, Mary Alice and I were at the Pink Pig in my rusty Ford station wagon. Our days of glamorous rides in a convertible were but a memory.

"I miss Bunny." Mary Alice was the first to verbalize how we all felt. "What do you think she's decided to do?"

"What I'd like to know," Misty said, "is how word got out so fast."

"I have a theory," I said. "Rumors start at the beauty shop and from there they go to the checkers at the Super Saver. They know everything, and they pass it on to every Tom, Dick and Harriette who comes through their line. Everyone in town eventually buys something at the grocery store, so it's like the Black Death. It spreads without mercy."

Misty and Mary Alice nodded and wisely kept quiet as the carhop placed the tray with our order on the window. I'd bet my bottom dollar the waitresses at the Pink Pig were another strand of the gossip web.

And speaking of gossip, Charlie strolled

over and jumped in the backseat with Mary Alice.

"Hey, M.A., how ya been?" he asked my friend.

"Fine, I'm just fine, thank you." When Mary Alice was nervous she reverted to what I called her Sunday-school manners, and Charlie was apparently making her very uneasy.

"Sunshine, do you think I could talk to you privately?" he asked.

"I, uh…" I was stalling, but I really didn't want a repeat of our conversation at the Chocolate Cow.

"Jazzy, give me your keys," Misty said. "You go with Charlie and I'll drive Mary Alice home. When you guys get through doing whatever you're gonna do, Charlie can bring you by my house to pick up your car."

Gee, thanks!

"Um, okay, I guess."

I followed him to his car with the enthusiasm of a condemned criminal.

We sat in silence for a few minutes before Charlie started the engine and pulled out of the lot. He had on his stubborn face, so I suspected he wasn't too interested in listening to anything I had to say—and that included asking about our destination. But the minute he turned toward the dam, I had a sinking feeling that I knew where we were headed.

Charlie parked on the gravel verge and he still hadn't said a word. The silent treatment was getting to me. Five more minutes and I was outta there. Even if I had to walk…

Yeah, right. Where Charlie was involved, I didn't have a lick of sense, and to add insult to injury, I couldn't resist temptation.

It wasn't until we were in Charlie's secret place that he got down to business.

"I want to apologize."

That one came out of left field. "Huh?"

"I…I realize you couldn't tell me Bunny's secret." Charlie shrugged, then continued his explanation. "The news hit me like a ton of bricks. I never knew I'd have such strong feelings about a baby." He shook his head. "It took me a while, but I've made peace with the fact that I'll never see my child—if there is one. That's something else I won't ever know."

He leaned back and closed his eyes. "I've never lost anyone important, so this was my first real experience with grief. I didn't handle it well. I'm sorry I jumped all over you. Friends?" He sat up and stuck out his hand as if to shake.

Bad, bad Jasmine—he wanted to shake hands and I was ready to jump his bones.

I was pitiful beyond belief.

It took me a ton of gumption, but I plastered a smile on my face. "Sure. We'll always be friends."

Chapter 10

The summer of '73 was racing to its conclusion. In three weeks I'd be packing for my big trip to California. Much as I hated to admit it, I was nervous. This was a life-changing event; my small-town Texas world would expand exponentially, and my carefree childhood would magically turn into adulthood, with all its responsibilities.

Charlie and I were both spending most of our time at the resort. I could understand his self-exile. The good folks of Meadow Lake were behaving like jerks. The way they were acting, you'd think he'd robbed a bank.

My motivation was a bit more ambiguous, even to me. Was I treating the resort as my home away from home because I wanted to be near Charlie? Or was I making an early separation from my friends in anticipation of my move?

I was sitting by the pool doing a mental inventory of my wardrobe when Charlie plopped down next to me.

"You want to head over to the café for a burger? I'll buy," he offered.

I pushed my sunglasses to the top of my head. "Will wonders never cease?" I asked. Oops, that was sarcastic. "Are you springing for French fries, too? Or will I have to cover that?" I gave him one of my best syrupy smiles. Served him right. He hadn't so much as waved to me in at least a week.

Charlie responded by pulling my ponytail. I was desperate for romance, roses and tender kisses, and what did he do? He fiddled with my hair, damn it. Who did he think I was, Cindy Brady?

"Come on, let's go." Charlie pulled me

out of my chair and pointed me in the direction of the restaurant's patio.

"And…I'll buy the fries." He laughed, and it sounded as if he'd made some wonderful joke. It reminded me why I'd fallen in love with him. It also made my heart ache, because our love was fated to end. It should be immortalized with all the great ill-starred love affairs—Romeo and Juliet, Antony and Cleopatra, Tristan and Isolde. Not that "affair" was really an accurate term for this relationship…

Comfort food was a useful concept—a greasy burger did make me feel better. I told myself that Charlie and I had known each other for years, plus, he'd been there for me throughout the boating disaster. So if he simply wanted to be friends, friends we'd be.

I wanted more—much more. That wasn't going to happen, but I didn't plan to abandon him when he needed me most.

"Have you heard from Bunny?" I asked. She hadn't contacted any of us and when I called her mother to get Bunny's address, Mrs. B. blew me off.

"No. How about you?"

"Not a word."

Charlie paused as if he was weighing what to say next. "We only had sex once. Bad luck, huh? As scuzzy as it makes me feel, I don't love Bunny. It was all about being a teenage boy." He gave me one of those smiles I couldn't resist. "Horny guys are a pretty irrational bunch."

"Hmm." What could you say to that? Be irrational with *me?*

I suppose he interpreted my response as an indication that he should continue. I wasn't sure I wanted to hear more.

"But you know what really hurts?"

"Hmm." As far as monosyllabic and completely noncommittal responses went, I guess that one was okay.

"She didn't respect me enough to even tell me she was pregnant. That baby's part of me, too. It's *my* baby!" Charlie smacked his chest. "Bunny and that *family* of hers decided I wasn't worthy enough to have an opinion."

He was right. The Bennetts had taken him completely out of the picture. Oh, the sins of the high and mighty.

"Charlie, I'm so sorry." I covered his hand and twined our fingers together. "I don't know what to say."

"Jaz, I don't mean to dump on you. Honest, I don't. But ever since I discovered what Bunny was up to, that's all I seem to think about."

"I don't blame you." Although I hated to refer to the gossip, I felt it was time to clear the air. "The way this town is treating you and Colton is unfair."

Charlie nodded in agreement. "I feel bad for my brother. He's an innocent victim." He threw me another one of those grins. "When Bunny and I were going hot and heavy, Colton was so jealous he couldn't see straight. Now, he's one of my biggest supporters. He wants to flip the bird to all the town biddies."

I'd pay ten bucks to see that.

"Come on, enough of this serious stuff. Let's go for a boat ride." I didn't have a chance to protest before he herded me down to the dock. I put on the brakes the moment I saw the same boat I'd been driving when the accident happened.

Charlie might be a kid, but he was insightful. "Let's make some good memories," he said.

That would be almost impossible, but if anyone could pull it off, it would be Charlie.

"Okay, I'm game, I guess."

He helped me into the boat and off we went for an afternoon in the sun. We stopped at his folk's fish camp first and loaded up on cold drinks and snacks. I'm sure he was working on the assumption that I wouldn't decline a cold Dr Pepper and a bag of Frito-Lay's with bean dip.

After we gathered our survival gear, aka junk food, we headed downriver to an island inhabited only by birds and a few water snakes. Charlie tied the boat to a tree stump, then we waded ashore to a small stretch of sandy beach.

"Do you remember in grade school, when you and Colton and I used to row over here to play?" he asked.

"How could I forget?" That memory was

from an idyllic summer before any of us realized there was a difference between boys
and girls.

"You two always ganged up on me."

"Yeah, well, we were kids."

We started our conversation sitting next
to each other on the blanket, but somehow, I
ended up on my back and Charlie was leaning over me. The kiss that began as a flutter
of light kisses quickly turned into a raging
inferno of teenage lust.

I loved him as only a seventeen-year-old
could. And miracle of miracles, I'm pretty
sure he felt the same. Charlie didn't verbalize his emotions, but it was there in the rev-
erence of his touch and the look on his face.
It was a validation of the relationship we'd
been moving toward for a very long time.

Since our adventure began at the swimming pool, I was wearing a T-shirt and a
pair of cutoffs over my bikini. Before I
could blink, Charlie made history of both
his shirt and mine, and was unbuttoning my
shorts. Not that I was complaining.

The friction of his bare skin against mine

was glorious and far beyond anything I'd ever imagined.

"Sunshine, what am I going to do with you?" Charlie muttered the rhetorical question as he unhooked the back of my bathing suit top.

As far as I was concerned, he could do whatever he desired—the faster the better.

When he slipped his fingers inside the elastic of my bikini bottom, I geared back my demand for faster and enjoyed the pleasure of slow and easy.

What we were doing went well beyond necking and petting and anything else in my repertoire.

For years, that afternoon in the sun and sand was a secret I brought out only when I had time to savor every delicious minute. We didn't consummate the deal, but we came pretty darned close.

With anyone else, I would've felt frightened or guilty or defiled. But this was Charlie, and that made all the difference in the world.

Chapter 11

The next morning, Bucky and I were down on the dock washing the lawn furniture. Yep, Bucky was back from camp and making my life miserable. That boy was worse than half the town's rumor divas.

Fortunately I'd perfected the art of ignoring him. If I pretended he wasn't there, I didn't have to deal with him. That way I could do something a lot more productive—like daydream.

Wash, scrub, rinse, conjure up visions of Charlie's gorgeous body. Not a bad way to spend a hot summer afternoon.

"Hey, Sunshine. You want to go for a ride?" Wow, that was weird. I hadn't heard Charlie's boat pull up to the dock.

"Bucky, you're invited, too," Colton said.

Bucky replied without glancing at either of the Morrison twins. "I don't think so."

Good grief, he sounded like Mama at her snottiest. It took everything I had not to smack him.

"Tell Mama I went out with Charlie and Colton, would you please?" I asked, putting on my best manners.

"You expect me to finish this chore by myself?"

"Get a grip, Bucky! We're almost done. It won't hurt you to spray off the last chair."

"It's not a good idea for you to go. With them."

That did it. I grabbed my brother's arm and towed him toward the lawn. "You're being a jerk. I'm leaving, so don't get your knickers in a twist."

It seemed like a fitting exit line, so I flounced off and jumped in the boat. Later on, I decided I should've been a bit more diplomatic.

* * *

"Jazzy, honey, it's so nice to see you," Mrs. Morrison said. Charlie's mom was her usual cheerful self. "You haven't been around in a month of Sundays."

She was doing her weekly baking and the kitchen smelled yummy. Mrs. Morrison made the best desserts in the whole county.

"I'm sorry I haven't been over lately," I said, sorely tempted to stick my finger in the cake batter.

"I've missed you." Mrs. Morrison patted my cheek before she took a batch of muffins from the oven. "Sit down. You can have one of these." She popped the hot pastries onto a cooling rack.

I didn't need a second invitation. Pigging out on hot muffins and cold milk was about as close to heaven as a mere mortal could get.

When our bellies were full, the twins and I wandered down to the river. We'd practically lived at the Morrisons' dock when we were kids. They had a water slide that guaranteed hours of fun.

"Are you ready for next year?" Colton asked.

My mother was usually ready to give someone the benefit of the doubt. On this topic, however, she'd completely flipped out.

I never, ever disobeyed my parents; that's because I was a charter member of the Goody-Two-Shoes club. This time I didn't care. Charlie and Colton were nice guys. They didn't deserve to be treated like lepers. I wasn't exactly sure who I was mad at— it could've been my family, Bunny's family or the whole community. Injustice was plain old wrong! And this was small-town discrimination at its worst.

I'd almost reached town before I decided on a destination. I was still boiling mad. And wow, I hated to even think about how much trouble I was going to be in when I got home, but I was on a mission.

The pay phone was inside the Pink Pig. That was about as private as the girls' locker room, but hey, I had to talk to Charlie, so my options were limited.

"I'm sorry your folks are in a tizzy," he said. "I didn't intend to get you involved in this mess."

Charlie had met me at our secret place. Notice how I'd assumed partial ownership.

"I haven't told you how important your friendship is to me." Charlie was playing with my hand, rubbing small circles on my palm. "That's a mistake I need to rectify." He moved his attention up to the tender skin of my inner arm.

"I have something else I want to tell you."

What now? Did he have a girlfriend stashed away in the next town?

"I've known for a while that you have a thing for me."

How embarrassing!

"I didn't say that to make you uncomfortable." By now Charlie was stroking the nape of my neck. "Way back when, I made a huge mistake and it was all Colton's fault." He chuckled as if he was amused.

In my opinion, there wasn't *anything* amusing about this conversation.

"Did you know that when we started high school, Colton was gaga over you?"

"Really?" That was a big surprise, although looking back, I think I suspected as much.

"Uh-huh." Charlie laughed again. "We got in a huge fight over you and I gave him a black eye. Do you remember that?"

"Yeah, you were grounded for a couple of weeks. But I didn't know you were fighting over me." I tried to dredge up the specifics from my memory. "In fact, I think you told me you guys were duking it out over who was going to ask Judy Champion to the dance. I also believe you said you were interested in her because she had boobs."

Charlie grinned at my acerbic observation. "You have to admit she was endowed."

"Yeah, whatever." I waved my hand in a gesture of dismissal.

"Anyway, I decided to back off and let Colton have an open field. The stupid dork didn't take advantage of his opportunity. Not that I would've had any better chance with you than he did."

Was he kidding? All he had to do was crook his finger and I'd have come running. But that was a little secret he didn't need to know.

Charlie was rubbing his hands up and

down my back, periodically making contact with bare skin.

"Colton and I were both smart enough to know you were out of our league."

"What?" With every one of his revelations, my voice elevated at least half an octave.

Charlie put on his best sheepish grin. "You're smart and funny and classy. We grew up in a fishing camp." He shook his head. "I'll bet you even know what to do with a pickle fork."

Talk about being thunderstruck. The Morrison twins had fought over me! And they thought I was too classy for them.

Unbelievable!

If I was so irresistible, not to mention sophisticated, why did I have to scrounge up my own prom date?

Charlie was running his fingers over my tummy. If he'd stopped, I would've been tempted to beat him senseless.

"I know this seems silly, but when I was treating you like a buddy it was a subterfuge for an emotion I didn't quite understand. You scared me to death. You still do."

When he replaced his fingers with his lips, I finally discovered what all the hoopla was about. Too bad I wasn't a kiss-and-tell kind of girl because boy, would I have a story!

Chapter 12

Our interlude signaled the end of my adolescence. It was also a turning point in my quest to become independent. So, as guilty as I felt, I took a page from Bunny's book and started sneaking around to see Charlie. Even though Mama was freaking out and Daddy was giving me the silent treatment, I wasn't deterred. No way in hell was I going to ditch Charlie. So there!

And that brought me full circle back to my errant blonde friend. I frequently thought about Bunny and wondered where she was and what she was doing. Whoever said your teenage years were the best time of your life was full of it.

The summer of 1973 had been a whirlwind of emotions, both tragic and euphoric. Now it was rapidly coming to a close and I had some big decisions to make. Did I really want to go to California? Or should I consider sticking closer to home—someplace like the University of Texas? Although I didn't confide in my parents, I think they realized something was afoot. But they were also more than willing to play ostrich.

To celebrate the end of summer, I invited Mary Alice and Misty to a sleepover at our guesthouse.

Misty lay on the couch, a bowl of popcorn in her hands. "I can't believe you ditched us for the past month. If we hadn't been friends forever, I'd be totally mad at you."

Mary Alice nodded in agreement.

They were right. I *had* been a terrible friend. Through no fault of their own, Misty and Mary Alice had first lost Bunny, and then I went MIA. I'd spent every spare minute with Charlie, talking, laughing, making out. That term—making out—was too casual, too ordinary, for what we did, even though I was still a virgin.

"Here's the deal." I sat down beside Misty and grabbed a few kernels of popcorn. "I might forget about Berkeley and go to UT."

"What?" my friends squealed. If I hadn't grabbed the bowl we would've had popcorn all over the floor.

"I called the registrar's office and asked them to send me an application. I didn't want Mama to see it, so I had it sent to your house." My comment was addressed to Misty. She'd already been accepted at UT, so a little more literature wouldn't raise any red flags.

"I thought maybe we could room together."

Misty snatched the bowl out of my hands. "Not that I wouldn't love having you as my roomie, but may I ask what bug got up your butt?"

I was hoping for more enthusiasm.

"They have a great school of architecture. It's close to home. And it's cheaper."

"That's BS," Misty responded. "This is all about Charlie, isn't it?"

Although Mary Alice didn't say a word, her eyes were the size of dinner plates. She obviously thought I was full of it, too.

And why should she believe me? It *was* a load of horse puckey. "The truth is I want to be with Charlie."

"I knew it! He's the reason you haven't been hanging out with us. You dirty dog! You've been keeping secrets from us. I want details and I want them now." Misty shot me one of her infamous glares.

One thing about knowing someone your entire life—you always knew when you couldn't win. So I gracefully conceded. "It's simple. I love him."

Three shrieks bounced off the walls. Good Lord, they were loud.

Misty started the questioning. "What does he think? Is it reciprocal?"

That was a good question. We'd never discussed anything permanent. What *were* his intentions? Unfortunately, I didn't have a clue.

"I, uh, I'm not sure."

I thought he cared about me. He acted like I was someone special. The problem was, he'd never actually uttered the three magic words.

"Whatever you decide to do, you know you can count on us," Misty said as Mary Alice nodded vigorously.

I was feeling as guilty as sin—not that I thought seeing Charlie was wrong. It was the sneaking around that bothered me. That didn't, however, negate my decision to ignore small-town prejudice.

Since we were attempting to keep our relationship a secret, our dates were limited to going out of town or spending time by the dam. That's where we were the night my life changed forever.

"What did you tell your folks?" Charlie asked. He wasn't immune to guilt, either.

"That Misty and I were going to the movies."

"Do you think they believed you?"

"Honestly, I don't know. It makes me feel bad to lie to them."

"I'm sorry about that. I don't want to come between you and your parents."

"They're both unreasonable."

Charlie had taken down my ponytail and was running his fingers through my hair.

"Have I mentioned how much I like your hair?"

He was darned good at the art of changing the subject.

"Uh-huh."

"How long has it been since you cut it?"

I wasn't quite sure. "Before we started high school. Probably four or five years ago."

"Hmm." He pulled a handful to his cheek and gently stroked it across his face. "I'm glad you didn't cut it."

Uh-huh—so was I.

Charlie let my hair slide through his fingers. I loved the way he touched me. Late at night when it was too hot to sleep I'd relive every one of our kisses. Over, and over and over again. Sometimes our kisses were sweet and lazy. At times they were hot and erotic, a sample of something that was far beyond my awareness of intimacy.

This time everything seemed different, more meaningful, somehow, than all our previous encounters.

Were we bonding through adversity? Or was this the excitement of the forbidden? In truth, it was probably a little of both, and a whole lot of love. Pure, unadulterated first love.

While Charlie teased me with his lips, alternating deep soulful kisses with playful nibbles, he inched his fingers up my back to the tie of my halter top. Moment by agonizing moment he worked on the knot until it fell open.

A cool breeze played across my nipples.

"Hmm." I was all but purring. And when his talented lips slid down my neck to feast on those nipples, I was lost. My common sense, my intellect, everything went *poof,* gone like dandelion fuzz in the breeze.

Summer days in south Texas could be, and usually were, wickedly hot. Add the humidity and, voilà, you had the makings of hell. But when the sun went down, the nights were magical. There were soft breezes. The bullfrogs and cicadas were singing. What more could a girl want? Hmm, not much.

And that's how I lost my heart and my virginity to a tall, blond Texas charmer. It wasn't something we planned. But *wink, wink*—when you mix teenage boys and sex you had the recipe for eternal optimism. And obviously he *was* optimistic, especially since he came prepared.

Bad boy, and another big wink!

I don't know what I expected, but making love was everything and nothing like I'd anticipated. It ran the gamut from incredibly embarrassing moments to a few chuckles. And everything in between. My only certainty was that it felt completely right.

Come hell or high water, Charlie was the love of my life.

Chapter 13

"I know what you and that Morrison kid were doing at the old pecan orchard." Bucky had just stuffed half a Pop Tart in his mouth when he dropped this bombshell.

Cool, I had to be cool. "Oh?" I continued to pour milk over my Frosted Flakes. "What was that?" There was no way he could *really* know what we did last night.

"I followed you and I saw Charlie's car parked next to yours."

I could hardly keep from hitting him. At times I dearly loved my brother. There were other times I'd gladly have been an only child.

"Mama's worried that you're gonna wreck your reputation." Bucky was wearing his concerned-older-brother face.

"For the sake of argument, what business is it of yours what I decide to do or who I decide to do it with?"

"Because, dummy, you're my sister and I love you." He cupped my face with his fingers. "And I happen to agree with Mama. You need to stay away from him. Besides—" he jammed the other half of the pastry in his mouth "—in two weeks you'll be on your way to California."

Little did he know! I'd sent my application to UT and I expected to hear from them any day. Mama and Daddy were not going to be happy when they found out what I'd done. And truly, it wouldn't have surprised me if they withheld their financial support. My ace in the hole was a small trust fund my grandmother had left me.

"I told Mom," Bucky said, barely suppressing a smirk.

That did it. I slammed the milk jug on

the table. "Great! That's just great. If you ever catch on fire, remind me not to spit on you." With that note of sarcasm floating in the air, I made a grand exit. Too bad it was to no avail.

I was almost at the stairs when I was hit right between the eyes by a maternal blast. "Jasmine Marie, I want to talk to you." Big uh-oh. The only time Mama used my full name was when I was in a load of trouble.

I trudged toward the living room.

"I know you've been sneaking out to see that kid."

Her tone of voice irritated me. "His name is Charlie," I muttered.

Typical of Mama, she acted as if she hadn't heard me. "I told you he was off-limits and you blatantly disobeyed me."

Mama rarely lost her temper, but when she did, she could compete with Mount Vesuvius. This time she looked like she was about to blow.

"You disobeyed me!" Her voice rose with each accusation. "And you used your friend to do it. I talked to Misty's mother. I am *so* disappointed in you."

What had happened to the "hear nothing, see nothing" routine they'd been practicing for the past couple of weeks?

Mama sank down on the couch, then issued the coup de grâce.

"Your daddy and I talked this morning and we decided you're grounded until you go to college. Give me your car keys."

She held out her hand as if I could miraculously produce the keys. I had on a pair of baby doll pajamas, for heaven's sake.

"I don't want you to see him or talk to him." She gave me the steely eye that always terrified the bag boys at the Super Saver, "And don't *consider* sneaking off."

Tears weren't usually part of my repertoire, not by a long shot, but I could feel them bubbling up. If she reacted like this about me seeing Charlie, she was going to have a stroke when I told her about my change of college plans. I quickly decided that announcement had to wait on the back burner, at least for the time being.

"Jasmine Marie, did you hear me?"

Everyone in a five-mile radius heard her.

"Yes, ma'am," I answered, barely managing to stifle my sarcastic tendencies.

I spent the rest of the day in bed, alternately sobbing and cussing. Growing up was not a job for wimps.

Two days later, Misty tapped on my bedroom door. "Your mom said I could come up," she said as she strolled in. "Gawd, girl, you look like crap."

"Thanks. I try." She was right. My hair was a tangled mess, my eyes were puffy from crying, and I hadn't bathed in all that time.

"Go take a shower, then we can talk," Misty demanded.

"You mean you don't want to smell this?" I raised my arm and headed in her direction. My sense of humor seemed to be returning.

"No," Misty squealed, edging around the end of the bed. "Go." She pointed in the direction of my bathroom.

"Okay," I conceded.

The rejuvenating power of hot water, shampoo and clean clothes combined to make me feel almost human.

"Let me tell you what happened." I started to explain when Misty stopped me.

"I know."

That had me putting on the mental brakes. "How do you know?"

She pulled a folded letter from the pocket of her cutoffs. "Believe it or not, Bucky called Charlie and told him. Guess he isn't such a bad brother after all. Anyway, since Charlie couldn't get to you any other way, he asked me to bring you this letter. I didn't read it. But if you want to talk after you've read it, I'm available."

She walked toward the door, but intuition told me to stop her. "Wait. I want to read it while you're here."

I read it, reread it, and then went through it again, hoping against hope for a different interpretation. I couldn't decide what to do, although I was leaning toward pitching a walleyed fit. What in the world was a walleyed fit, anyway?

But instead of freaking out, I crumpled the letter and threw it into the wastepaper basket. Too bad it wasn't Charlie's head. Misty, bless her heart, was *dying* to pull it out of the trash and read it. Lord, that girl had a ton of self-restraint.

A cynical chuckle managed to sneak past my defenses. "I'll put you out of your misery and tell you what it said."

"Well, spill it," she ordered as she stacked my pillows against the headboard while I paced.

"Charlie said we need to start college life without any high-school baggage. Baggage, my butt! How dare he?" Thinking about the letter was enough to make me homicidal, but I controlled myself. "It was a short and sweet 'have a nice life' letter. He can burn in hell!"

I was feeling a bit more violent than I'd thought. "If that's what he wants, that's what he'll get. As far as I'm concerned, he has ceased to exist."

Misty wore one of her doubtful looks.

"Well, he has. He's the biggest idiot on the face of the earth."

I wasn't about to shed another tear for someone who thought I was baggage. Baggage!

* * *

As I snapped the lock on my last suitcase I had a wonderful epiphany. Somehow I'd made it through a painful trial on the journey to becoming an adult.

Charlie was one of life's hard lessons for me. It was time to brush myself off and say so long to my childhood and my first love.

Hello, California.

Hello, future.

Summer 1993

Chapter 14

High-school reunions were a scourge, and the class of 1973's twentieth reunion was no exception. Someone, probably Mary Alice, had come up with the mother of all hare-brained schemes. Our senior year was during the wind-down of the Vietnam War, and as the ultimate PC gesture we'd decided to forgo a prom. Instead of getting all dolled up in corsages and bow ties, we'd donated our class funds to a local animal shelter.

At the time we considered it a noble gesture—and it was. But as the years passed, one of our classmates, or more than likely several of them, decided they'd been cheated out of a critical rite of adolescent passage—a prom.

Mary Alice initiated her telephone campaign in late May and, bless her heart, she was relentless. I'd been dodging phone calls from Mary Alice for weeks. Then she got wise and resorted to using my voice mail. That girl was no dummy.

"You were the class secretary, so you have an obligation to be here. Call me when you get home. I mean it!" Mary Alice's previous three messages expressed an identical sentiment. The only thing she changed was the extent of the wheedling and begging. But no matter how guilty I felt about ignoring her, I wasn't going to return her call. My mama hadn't raised a dummy, either.

The very thought of a reunion was enough to send cold chills up and down my spine. And the idiot who'd dreamed up a "prom" at the Moose Lodge, complete with long dresses and rented tuxes, deserved a lobotomy or worse.

I was doing just fine, thank you very much. I did not need a relapse into puberty.

As an architect I'd hit the big time. My style was stamped on hotels in Thailand, retirement communities in Mexico and ski resorts in Colorado.

I was happy. My career was going well. I had a honkin' big diamond on my left hand. And I was BSing myself. There was something missing in my life and I wasn't sure what that was. I suspected it was laughter, but considering the fact that I hadn't had a good belly laugh since 1990, what did I know?

"Jasmine, could we go over the drawings for the Vista Del Sol project?" The speaker was Dominic Rinaldi, my business partner and fiancé. He was standing in my office door holding a roll of blueprints.

"Okay," I answered. "Come on in." Considering our relationship, it was odd that he never entered my personal space without an invitation. That seemed to signify an emotional gap between the two of us, and I was afraid that was the root of my discontent.

"Dad wants to meet us for lunch sometime this week." He strolled over to the minibar to pour a glass of Perrier.

"I'd love to have lunch with Santo." Not only was Professor Santo Rinaldi Dom's father, he was also one of my dearest friends. For years he'd been my surrogate California dad. "I haven't seen him in a couple of weeks. What's he been up to?"

Dom answered with a noncommittal shrug. With my fiancé, that could mean anything from he didn't know to he didn't want to bother telling me. To be honest, there were a lot of things about Dom that puzzled me.

But getting back to Santo, I met him during my freshman year when I took a part-time job as his administrative assistant. Talk about a fiasco. My office skills were nonexistent, and to make matters worse, I was so homesick I cried constantly.

It took almost six weeks for Santo to finally give me a pink slip. That was the bad news; the good news was that he became my mentor. When his wife, Martha, was alive I spent more time at their home than I did at my apartment. She claimed I was the daughter of her heart.

In hindsight, I'm fairly sure the Rinaldis were praying I'd fall in love with their son and make my honorary family status official. When Dom got married, he temporarily thwarted those plans, but after his divorce Santo went into full matchmaker mode. So guess what? Their wish was about to come true.

Dom and I started out as friends, progressed to a business partnership and then, with Santo's encouragement, segued into engagement. I knew my biological clock was bonging like crazy, but I'd been so professionally oriented that during the past twenty years I hadn't put much emphasis on relationships. Not that I hadn't had boyfriends; I had, but once they got serious, I dumped them.

First and foremost, I was a career woman. But on the rare occasion when I was completely honest with myself, I had to admit I'd never stopped loving Charlie. Not only that, he played a starring role in my dreams with disturbing frequency. *Enough of that!* I always told myself, trying not to think of him. I was successful and I was happy. Was I protesting too much?

Our architectural firm was successful beyond our dreams. Initially Santo had provided the seed money and moral support, and throughout the lean years he was our guardian angel. I doubt very much that we could've made it without him.

But make it we did. The Bay Area was fertile ground for our brand of land use planning and eventually we flourished.

I was still thinking about Santo as Dom prattled on.

"I have to fly to Costa Rica in the morning and I'd like you to check the preliminaries. We've followed all the regulations, but I'm still concerned about the local officials," he commented as he rolled out the schematics.

He should be worried. Dealing with a Central American bureaucracy was at best a capricious situation.

"I spoke to the project manager yesterday and he tells me that everything's under control." I tried to reassure him as I sat down at my drafting table. The Vista Del Sol resort was our key to architectural stardom. If—no, *when*—we pulled this off, we'd be in the rarified atmosphere of Duany and Plater-Zyberk, the gurus of New Urbanism architecture.

I studied Dom as he went into a monologue on street widths, lot sizes and ocean views. No doubt about it, he was a handsome man. His blue-black hair and brown eyes were courtesy of his Italian ancestry. As I fingered the two-carat diamond on the third finger of my left hand, I wondered, as I frequently did, what was missing.

It had to be the innate difference between male and female thought processes. He was talking about business while I was contemplating our relationship, our living situation, and the fact that we had nothing in common outside the office. We shared a bed, a home and even a mortgage, but our personal interactions were strangely sterile.

Then it hit me like a brick. Our conversations were always centered on work. That was pitiful!

Had I accepted Dom's proposal because I loved him or because Santo kept pushing us together? Deep down I realized we didn't have that magical spark, but we had everything else going for us. And in the overall scheme of things, "falling in love" was highly overrated. Wasn't it?

Or was I simply comparing everyone to Charlie?

That niggle of doubt spurred me to make a decision.

"Dom, since you have Villa Del Sol under control and I don't have anything else that's pressing, I'm going to Texas." I'd been complaining about the reunion for weeks, so my pronouncement came as a huge surprise to both of us.

"Are you sure?" he asked.

"Yes, I'm positive." And I really was. It was time to cast out some of my demons. I glanced at the ring and immediately thought of Charlie. He was the first demon I planned to exorcise. If I could do that, perhaps I could get him out of my dreams.

Unfortunately, that might be easier said than done.

Chapter 15

When I finally called Mary Alice and accepted the invitation, I discovered that Misty was coming but Charlie, Colton and Bunny were missing in action. Mary Alice wasn't sure they'd even received the invitation. So exactly why was I making the trip?

The Red Carpet Room at the Denver airport provided a haven of quiet in the midst of the hectic horde of summer travelers. It had been a frenetic day. Before seven o'clock my office manager had called with the crisis du jour, and now my connection to

San Antonio was delayed because of thunderstorms.

I still couldn't believe I'd agreed to attend a *prom* at the Moose Lodge. I had, however, put my foot down on the prom-dress idea. Taffeta and tulle—was Mary Alice completely demented?

I was professional, I was sophisticated, I was confident, and who was I trying to fool? Sometimes my twang surfaced at the most inopportune times. At heart, I was still a small-town Texas girl.

I was watching a cowboy in a Stetson drinking Jack Daniel's when someone stood in front of me.

"Sunshine, is that really you?"

Where was a defibrillator when a person needed one? That baritone couldn't belong to anyone but Charlie Morrison. I got to my feet and looked reluctantly into the most gorgeous green eyes I'd ever seen—eyes I'd remember if I lived to be a hundred.

Before I could contemplate fate's twisted sense of humor I was enveloped in a hug. It was an embrace that evoked lustful memories of soft summer nights. That was *not* good. What was it about this man that got under my skin, even after all the years?

"Charlie," I gasped, almost breathless as I disengaged myself. "Charlie." So what happened to my professional demeanor?

"That's my name." He laughed as he sat down on an adjacent chair. "You look fantastic. I knew you'd be a stunning woman."

Speaking of *stunning*. He'd grown into his body—boy, had he ever grown into his body. As a teenager he was tall and lanky; as an adult he was broad shouldered and built like a pro athlete. And his shaggy blond hair and tan still reminded me of a California surfer.

I was trying to come up with a scintillating response or at the very least something polysyllabic, but Charlie beat me to the punch.

"I've kept up with you through my mom." He gave a short laugh. "I hear you're a hotshot architect with a practice in San Francisco."

Mama, darn her hide, hadn't bothered to mention the Morrison brothers— not once—in all these years. Could it be because I didn't ask her? It wasn't as if I hadn't thought about them. In fact, I wondered about Charlie almost to the point of obsession. I'd even considered asking Mary Alice, but then I chickened out.

As much as I loved Mama, she was a snob. She dismissed the Morrisons' fish camp as nothing more than a beer joint. So when I made my summer pilgrimages home I rarely visited Charlie's mom, although she was one of my very favorite people. But I always went out to the old dam to think and remember. It was still my special place.

"I'm sorry." I gripped my wineglass. "You have me at a disadvantage. I don't know what you've been doing."

Charlie's deep laugh sent chills skittering up my spine. "We didn't part on the best of terms, so I'm not surprised you put me out of your mind."

Oh, but I hadn't been able to put him out of my mind. In fact, I thought about him, dreamed about him and periodically had fantasy conversations with him. It was impossible to forget the person who took your virginity—and your heart.

"I really do like your hair." He twirled a strand of my pageboy around his finger. He used to love playing with my hair.

"And the duds are cool, too."

I couldn't decide whether he was serious or not. I hadn't bothered to change before I headed to the airport, so I was still wearing one of my power suits. It wasn't what you'd call seduction attire. But who said anything about seduction?

"Thanks. I suppose." I'd finally regained the ability to form a coherent sentence. "Why don't you give me a synopsis of the past twenty years?"

"Synopsis, huh?"

When he grinned, it took me back to another time and place. Then I noticed my ring. The diamond was so big and glittery it was hard to miss, but for a few seconds Dominic had ceased to exist. Big *uh-oh!*

"I'm a pediatrician. I have a practice here in Denver."

"Really? That's great." It was also astonishing. I'm not sure why that thought crossed my mind. Although he'd told me he wanted to be a doctor, I hadn't realized he was planning to specialize in children.

A sad look momentarily crossed Charlie's face. It was replaced by an expression I couldn't quite understand. "It all started with Bunny that summer of our senior year." He shrugged. "The whole experience made me want to help kids, be involved with them. I guess it's related to—almost—being a father when I was just a kid myself. If that makes any sense…"

In the annals of uncomfortable topics, this was a doozy. How could Bunny completely ignore Charlie's feelings and then prance off to an exclusive girls' school as if she didn't have a care in the world?

Regrettably, that's exactly what she'd done. Several years after that ill-fated summer, Mama heard at a bridge party that Bunny had miscarried. I wondered whether Charlie was privy to that information.

"Did you hear what happened to the baby?"

Charlie shook his head. "No. I asked everyone in town. My mom tried to find out and Colton got in touch with all his sources, but we were stonewalled. After I started making money, I even hired a private investigator. He found Bunny, but he never discovered any information about the child."

"She miscarried."

He nodded. "I suspected it was something like that. There wasn't any record, so I knew it was either a miscarriage or a private adoption—or an abortion. But, somehow, I couldn't imagine Bunny terminating the pregnancy. I'm glad I know what happened. At least now I won't be looking for some twenty-year-old with a family resemblance."

It was time to change the subject. "And what's Colton doing?"

The non sequitur wasn't lost on Charlie. "He's a family attorney in Dallas. The black-sheep Morrison boys did a whole lot better than the town expected. He's married and has four of the cutest little rug rats you've ever seen."

"That's nice." I was usually adept at small talk. This situation, however, had ruined my composure.

"How about you?" he asked. Then he apparently saw the ring, because he paused and stared at the diamond.

"I'm engaged to my business partner. We plan to get married next year." Actually we hadn't discussed a date, but I didn't see any need to go into that source of irritation.

"And you?"

"Never been married, never been engaged." He waggled his fingers in the air indicating the lack of a ring. Then he moved on to another topic. "I haven't been in touch with any of our classmates. This is going to be weird."

That was my feeling, too.

"Colton's not planning to show. He's not too fond of Meadow Lake. His actual words were 'over my dead body.' Guess he doesn't believe in equivocating, huh?"

His comment merited a laugh. "I guess not."

"So how about hanging out with me? For old times' sake?"

That would be a huge mistake. But for this brief weekend, this ephemeral moment,

I craved a taste of childhood. I wanted to go home again.

"Okay, I'd love to spend some time with an old friend."

Chapter 16

During my early years in California I made the effort to go home every summer, although I never stayed long. Later, it seemed easier for my parents to visit me, especially since Daddy was retired and they had time to travel. Consequently, I was out of touch with the pace of life in Meadow Lake.

I was still in a delightful fog of sleep when I heard the phone ring. Not to worry, Mama would get it, I thought as I snuggled down in the bedding. Being home was actually kind of nice. Drifting off to sleep was even better.

The next thing I knew, Mama was standing by the bed with a glass of orange juice in one hand and the cordless phone in the other.

"Mary Alice is on the line," she said, handing me the receiver. "Breakfast is on the table."

"Okay, I'll be down in a minute," I told her, taking the phone.

"Hey, Mary Alice, what's up?"

"I am *so* excited you're here." Her squeal was so loud I was afraid I'd have permanent hearing damage. "Petey and I had a bet going that you wouldn't show. I won't tell you what he has to pony up. Silly man." I hadn't heard her giggle like that since we were in junior high. Oh, to be that happy. And why not? Mary Alice and Petey were one of the best-suited couples I'd ever met.

The only memory I could dredge up about their wedding back in 1976 was the god-awful bilious-green bridesmaid's dress I was forced to wear. At the time I couldn't quite decide whether I looked like a dead frog or a giant radioactive mushroom. In retrospect, I think I'd have to give my vote to the deceased amphibian. Considering Mary Alice's fashion choices at the time, her taste had obviously improved. Because, believe it or not, Miss "I Couldn't Accessorize If My Life Depended On It" owned the trendiest dress shop in town. She probably even knew the difference between puce and cerise.

"Yeah, well, it was touch and go for a while. But I'm here, so how are you going to keep me busy?" I really didn't expect anyone to entertain me; I just thought it would be fun to pull Mary Alice's chain.

"You'll never guess who called me last night."

Oh, yes, I could.

"Charlie Morrison's in town. Can you *believe* it?" Although Mary Alice had been privy to some of my angst concerning Charlie, she didn't realize the importance of our liaison twenty years ago.

"I know. I ran into him at the Denver airport. We were on the same flight."

"No kidding!" She squealed again.

Good grief. Someone should tell her about the dangers of high-decibel noise pollution.

"So if I invite you both to a barbecue tonight, you'll come?"

I'm sure she was shocked by my quick answer. "Of course. All that high-school stuff is water under the bridge."

Or was it? I guess I'd find out this weekend.

"Great. Come over about five-thirty and bring your bathing suit." She giggled. "Petey's doing all the cooking. Ever since I bought the store, he's been a doll about housework."

Sweet, sweet Petey—he was a keeper.

"And why don't you come by and kidnap me for lunch? We've got a bunch of catchin' up to do."

"I'll pick you up around noon. Is that okay?"

Before she could answer, there was a wail in the background.

"Gotta go. Daisy and Blossom are fighting over the puppy's chew toy. See you soon."

Before I could nod or grunt or anything else, she was gone. Mary Alice's three girls were all named for flowers, so I wasn't positive which one of the combatants was the kid and which the dog.

Mama's idea of a light breakfast was golden French toast with warm syrup and crispy bacon. Yikes! If she kept up this food orgy, I'd be waddling home. Fortunately I had my running shoes. I'd just stuffed a piece of toast in my mouth when she launched into the last topic I wanted to discuss.

"I saw Anita Morrison at the Super Saver the other day."

That wasn't surprising since the supermarket was the epicenter of town gossip. Everyone, and I do mean everyone, hit the Super Saver at least once a week.

"She said Charlie's going to be in town for the reunion. Did you know that?"

I could avoid the question, but I decided not to. Several years following the summer fiasco, I began to suspect that Mama and Daddy had something to do with Charlie's abrupt change of heart. I wasn't inclined to explore that topic, however, choosing instead to go with the concept that ignorance was bliss.

So rather than elaborating on a touchy subject, I gave her the same story I'd given Mary Alice. Coward that I was, I refused to analyze the feelings that our serendipitous Denver meeting had evoked. It was obvious he was over me, but it was even more obvious that I wasn't immune to him, even though I was engaged.

That was a huge problem, I thought as I twirled the large solitaire. Could I really treat him like a buddy when I still had vivid and erotic dreams about him? Heaven help me—Charlie was more tempting than a hot-fudge sundae with whipped cream.

A long run cleared my mind and I was ready to take on twenty years' worth of gossip. Mary Alice was now the society maven of Meadow Lake. Darn, that was incredible.

Petey had started in the school system as the band director and quickly worked his way up to high-school principal. I suppose his ultimate destination was the superintendent's office. Underneath his quiet facade he was very goal-oriented. Look at the way he'd pursued Mary Alice.

Between the two of them, they were involved in every civic organization in town. Sweet little Mary Alice a mover and shaker—who would've guessed?

The boutique was housed in a bright-yellow Victorian resplendent with white gingerbread trim and green shutters. The inside decor was as appealing as the outside. It was a delightful combination of class and kitsch.

Although Mary Alice and I periodically talked on the phone, it'd been several years since we'd actually seen each other, and wow, what a difference. She looked polished, with fashionably short hair and subtle jewelry, and she was wearing some seriously expensive clothes. But thank goodness, she was still the same wonderful person.

After giving me a big hug, she introduced me to her staff and then pulled me out the door into the sweltering heat. I'd almost forgotten what summer in south Texas could be like. It was hell, with a capital *H*.

"How do you guys stand this?" I asked, wiping off my sunglasses. The sudden temperature change from the air-conditioned boutique to the steamy outdoors had created a fog problem.

"What are you talking about?"

Bless her heart.

"This." I waved a hand at the shimmering heat rising from the asphalt.

For a second Mary Alice seemed puzzled. "Oh, you mean how hot it is?" She didn't wait for an answer before she broke into giggles. "We're not into the steamy season yet. I think you've been away too long. It's *so* good to have you back." She made that pronouncement with more confidence than I felt.

"Girl," she went on, "I think you need some Mexican food, and Alberto's is the perfect spot for our first get-together. It's down on the river, close to where we went skinny-dipping." She chuckled. "Do you remember when we did that?"

In a long list of memories it was definitely one that stood out. "I remember." I was feeling so comfortable listening to her prattle, I didn't elaborate on the feelings that memory evoked. Maybe it *was* possible to go home again, I thought as I followed her to her car, a Volvo station wagon—the appropriate vehicle for an up-and-coming society matron.

After we'd placed our order at Alberto's and the tortilla chips and salsa arrived, I got brave enough to ask her about the old gang. I'd been remiss in keeping up with anyone. When Mary Alice and I had one of our periodic telephone conversations, we mostly talked about our jobs and families.

"What's Misty doing now?" I figured she'd be a safe person to start with. After all, Misty had been voted the most likely to succeed. She'd gone to law school and then joined a large firm, but I hadn't heard anything about her recently.

Uh-oh. That might not have been an accurate assumption, not if the look on Mary Alice's face was any indication.

"Hmm." She shoved a chip in her mouth.

I recognized a stall when I saw one. I was a master of that particular tactic. I should be; I used it frequently enough with Dom.

"Spill it."

"She's the District Attorney of Austin."

"Wow! That's great." Austin was the political center of Texas. And District Attorney was a plum elected position.

"I didn't know she had political aspirations." There were obviously a *lot* of things I didn't know about my old friends.

"I'm not sure she did, not until a couple of years ago," Mary Alice said, sipping her margarita. "Something happened and I have no idea what it was, but it really changed her. She's, uh, well, she has a hard edge now." M.A. shrugged. "You'll see what I'm talking about this evening. She'll be at the barbecue. In fact, Misty's spending the night at our house. I'm sure it won't surprise you that she's not on very good terms with her parents."

"No, that doesn't surprise me. It'll be wonderful to see her."

"Yeah, well." Mary Alice wrinkled her nose. I wasn't sure what that meant. I didn't think it was anything positive.

Then her expression brightened as she filled me in on the exploits of our classmates, some of whom I barely remembered. The big omission in her recap of twenty years was Bunny.

"What about Bunny? Do you know where she lives?" I asked when Mary Alice finally ran out of steam.

"The last I heard, she was in New York with her second husband." She paused as if she was retrieving information from her brain's data bank. "He's some kind of hotshot stockbroker. She didn't respond to the invitation, so I seriously doubt we'll be seeing Bunny."

Although my curiosity was working overtime, I suspected her absence would be a blessing. Especially considering that the primary reason I'd come home was to sort out my feelings for Charlie. Did I love Dom? Or did I accept a ring from him because of my loyalty to his father—and because the man I really wanted was lost to me twenty years ago?

One good thing about being home was that I had time to think. After seeing Charlie, I knew deep in my heart that my feelings for him hadn't abated.

Would they ever change? That's what I had to decide.

Chapter 17

I staked out a prime spot by the pool and was watching eight-year-old Lily and five-year-old Rose do cannonballs into the pool. Over and over again the little imps jumped into the water, squealing at the top of their lungs. I was about to max out on that activity when a tall, dark-haired hunk made himself at home on the deck chair beside mine.

"Hey, Jazzy, you're looking good."

So was he. Too bad I didn't have a clue who *he* was. "So are you." He was obviously someone I'd known, but without a name tag—and may I say that pasting anything on that nice hairy chest would be a crime—I was outta luck.

Fortunately he had a sense of humor. "You don't recognize me, do you?"

"No. I don't." I hoped he appreciated honesty.

He leaned back in the chair and gave me a once-over. "Do you remember getting drunk in a '57 Plymouth?"

"Oh, my God," I squealed. Was squealing communicable? "Don't tell me you're Billy Tom."

"Guilty as charged. But I go by Bill now."

"You've, uh, you've, uh—" Okay, I was rendered speechless.

"Grown up?"

"Yep, you've grown up." Ooh, yeah.

We'd begun the "what are you doing these days" parley when Misty approached. Swear to goodness, if I'd run over her in my car I'm not sure I would've recognized her.

Misty was gorgeous in an anorexic-model kind of way. She was impeccably dressed and the mop of beautiful red that usually ran riot was scraped back into an intricate chignon. Her entire appearance was disconcerting, but the thing that really blew me away was her eyes. When we were kids she had a sparkle that was infectious. It was missing. She had this "don't mess with me" aura that was almost palpable.

Bill stood when she approached. The man had manners. When had that happened? Apparently he caught the same vibe I did, because he didn't attempt to tease her.

"Hi, Misty. I don't know if you remember me. I'm Bill Jackson. Billy Tom." He extended his hand and when she ignored him he pulled it back and did an abbreviated wave. He put on one of those good-old-boy grins. "I live in Austin, too."

Her lack of response was eloquent.

"I'm the head of the DEA office," he said, still trying to draw her into a conversation.

"Yes, I know. Nice seeing you." Her words were cold as ice. "And Jazzy," she added before strolling off, "I'm glad you came. Let's talk later."

"What was *that* about?" I asked. Charlie had walked up in time to hear Misty's parting remark.

"Beats me," Bill answered, echoing what we were all obviously thinking.

"That woman's got the bitch act down pat," Bill commented, slapping Charlie on the back. "Hey, big guy, long time no see."

"Twenty years. I'd say that's a long time, all right. And not to offend you or anything, but you're the last guy I ever thought would end up being a cop."

Bill wasn't insulted; in fact, he broke into a belly laugh. "The wild ones do the best in my line of work. It takes one to know one."

The guys were well into typical male bonding, reminiscing about high-school antics, particularly the infamous '57 Plymouth booze binge, when Petey abandoned the barbecue pit and joined us. Petey had been such a sweet guy in high school that he was at a loss for anything to add.

A girl could take only so much testosterone, so I wandered over to where Misty was sitting in the shade. I have to admit I approached her with trepidation. I didn't know whether she was mad at me or whether she had it in for the whole world.

"Hi, Jazzy, I'm glad you came. Mary

Alice didn't know if you'd make it or not."
She smiled and for a minute she was the
Misty I knew and loved. Then it was as if
she remembered something awful and her
entire demeanor changed.

"You're looking good," I responded. And
if you discounted her scowl, she was gorgeous, way too thin, but still beautiful.
Mama would love to feed her.

"Thanks. So are you. Very professional."

That wasn't exactly what I wanted to accomplish with my sleek one-piece suit. For
once in my life I'd like someone, anyone, to
say I was sophisticated or, better yet, sexy.
Just like Misty in her barely-there floral
two-piece with matching sarong.

"I'm sorry about the way I acted. That
was inexcusably rude. I didn't even say hi.
I'm very embarrassed."

Before I could speak, she continued. "For
some reason, he gets under my skin. I know
who he is, of course, although I've never
worked with him. In our business it's hard
to miss the major players."

That was interesting. When we were
kids we shared everything. Now it was

hard to have a discussion without a plethora of pauses. Maybe Mary Alice was right. Something bad *had* happened to Misty, and I'd bet a dollar to a doughnut that it involved a man.

I wanted to delve further into that mystery, but my cell phone jingled. Darn, I should've turned it off.

Darn again. It was Dom.

"Hello, Jasmine." Before I'd said a word, he launched into a series of questions related to work. Just what I needed when I was at a party. But I gave him the information he requested.

Then he got down to the real reason he'd called. "I thought you might want to know that Father is sick."

Might want to know? Might want to know! I took a deep breath. "How sick is he?"

"He's in the hospital, but I haven't been over to see him yet. I've been too busy."

"You've been too busy." I told myself not to scream an obscenity. That would send my fiancé into the passive-aggressive mode I hated.

"Give me the number of the hospital and I'll call him." That way I'd get information that wasn't filtered through Dom's unique perspective. "Are you still planning to go to Costa Rica?"

"Of course."

Of course. What was I thinking?

When I dialed the hospital, I was immediately connected to Santo's room. He assured me it was nothing more than the flu and told me I shouldn't be concerned. His exact words were "*Bambina,* don't worry about this old man. You have fun with your friends." That was easier said than done, especially now.

"I didn't mean to eavesdrop, but it was difficult not to hear your conversation," Misty said. "Is everything all right?"

"I don't know. I guess so." I took a big slurp of my drink. "My future father-in-law's in the hospital so I'm feeling guilty about being here. We're very close. I'm not sure I'm getting all the facts about his condition."

"Don't worry, he'll be fine." Misty patted my hand and took my glass to refill it.

* * *

After several margarita refills, I was feeling no pain. Bill and Charlie were sneaking worried glances at me. Silly boys, they thought I didn't notice what they were doing. Another hiccup-giggle broke loose when Charlie tried to surreptitiously remove my glass.

"Come on, Jazzy. I'm taking you home," he said, marching me toward the patio doors. "Say goodbye, Petey."

"Goodbye, Petey." I was one of those happy drunks who did everything with a smile. Not that I got tipsy very often; in fact, I can count those occasions on one hand.

"Do you remember the night Billy Tom took you girls to the drive-in?"

"Of course." I tried to be serious and ruined it with a snicker.

"Bucky and I were trying to control the situation, and you all just got louder and louder."

"It was funny, wasn't it?"

"I'm not sure I'd say that. By the way, where *is* good old Bucky?"

"He's a judge down in Kingsville. Isn't that the strangest thing you've ever heard?"

Charlie laughed and that encouraged me to serenade him with stanza after stanza of our high-school song. Poor Charlie— I didn't know many of the words and my singing voice was enough to send small children running in fear.

"We're home." He pulled up behind the infamous bougainvillea.

"Really," I giggled. "And I'm not puking petals." My adroit observation merited another round of hysterical laughter. "Petals, get it?"

Even in my incapacitated state I could tell he wasn't the happiest camper in town, so I decided to make him lighten up. Bad idea— especially since my brilliant plan included a kiss. Why not? I *had* loved him forever.

"Jaz." He held me at arm's length. "You know I love you, and the only reason I'm telling you that is because you won't remember it in the morning." His smile was so tentative and lovable I launched myself at him again.

"Darn, you're cute," he muttered before he turned me around and marched me straight to the back door.

"If your mama asks, tell her I'm not responsible for this debacle," he added.

The day was turning into a living, breathing hell, and all because I had the second hangover of my life. Please God, would someone take pity and put me out of my misery.

For some reason I thought that sitting by the pool at the resort sipping an icy Coke would be restorative. It wasn't. The Coke was tepid, the sun was searing and a gaggle of kids were playing Marco Polo. Could this day get any worse?

Yes, it could.

"Hey, Sunshine, do you have a headache?" I flipped up my sunglasses and shot Charlie one of my best drop-dead glares.

"I'm not exactly feeling chipper." Making a fool of yourself in front of people you hadn't seen in *twenty years* was humiliating enough. Having some guy gloat about it was unbearable.

My response drew a hoot of laughter. "So

I can't talk you into going with me to the Sonic for a chili cheese dog, huh?"

He was a very evil man. "Shut! Up!"

He laughed even harder. "Sorry, I couldn't resist." He leaned back in the chaise and watched the kids cavort. "You know," he said. "I like kids."

Talk about tugging at the heartstrings. "I know."

He nodded, but didn't say anything else. We were skirting a touchy subject.

"Let's go have some fun tomorrow. What do you say?"

I'd say that sounded *way* too good. Was he asking me on a date? I was engaged, but I'd decided to think about that later. After all, this was nothing more than an innocent interlude. Old friends getting together. Uh-huh, I almost had myself convinced—until my little inner voice piped up.

That twit was a real spoilsport!

South Texas provided an abundance of adult, sophisticated date venues; unfortunately, Charlie hadn't selected one. Nope,

Wildly Wet was a gigantic water park, a mecca to throngs of nubile adolescents.

"Do you really think I'm going out there," I waved my hands in a gesture that encompassed the parking lot, the town, the county and, yep, the whole world, "and show off my aging body in a bathing suit? No siree, not this girl."

Charlie gave me the same grin that had captured my seventeen-year-old heart. Unfortunately, my thirty-eight-year-old heart was just as susceptible. He pulled into an open parking spot, but didn't turn off the car or the air conditioner.

"It'll be fun, I promise." Much to my surprise, Charlie picked up my hand and kissed the base of each finger. This felt more and more like a date, and it seemed so right.

"Um, well." He was wearing down my resistance and he knew it. "Okay, I guess."

And it *was* okay. Better than okay. It turned out to be the most fun I'd had in years.

We slid down miles and miles of water-slick tubes, rode a boogie board in the wave pool and lounged around the man-made beach. I even took some god-awful ride that catapulted screaming people halfway to Mars.

I knew that in the morning my muscles would be screaming and, considering our junk-food orgy, my tummy would be doing somersaults. We gorged ourselves on a veritable smorgasbord of high-calorie and low-nutrition snacks—from corn dogs to florescent-yellow nachos and Sno-Kones to roasted turkey legs. The way I was giggling and playing with Charlie, I felt like I was seventeen again.

Too bad my thighs weren't circa 1973.

Chapter 18

Oh. My. Gawd! Now I remembered. Too much fun, too much sun, too much whatever had major next-day consequences.

As I rolled over, I caught a glimpse of my arm and instantly realized why I was so miserable. I was parboiled.

"Crap!" I was about to launch into a tirade of expletives when my cell phone rang. "What?"

I'd never been much of a morning person, but today I'd turned into Cruella De Vil's evil twin.

"Hey, Sunshine. How do you feel?"

"How do you think I feel?" I snapped. This disaster wasn't Charlie's fault, so I shouldn't be taking out my bad humor on him. Somehow, I couldn't help myself.

"I think you're sunburned."

"The tops of my toes are singed," I wailed. I don't know what I thought he could do about it, but he *was* a doctor.

"Do you have any vitamin E capsules?"

"Yes." I flopped back on the bed and continued inspecting the damage I'd done to my body—my poor, whale-belly-white body. I'd used a ton of sunblock, really I had.

"Cut a bunch of those capsules open and spread the liquid all over your skin. I guarantee it'll make you feel better. We're supposed to have dinner tonight with Mary Alice and Petey, remember?"

In all my misery I'd forgotten. "I don't know if I can do that." Actually I wasn't quite sure I could face wearing a bra.

"Use the vitamin E. I promise it'll work." He chuckled before he dispensed the next bit of medical advice. "Take two aspirin and give your doc a big sloppy kiss the next time you see him."

"Uh-huh." Even though my sense of humor was seriously compromised, I found myself laughing with him.

"Have a nap this afternoon and call me when you get up. I want to see you, okay?"

"Okay," I agreed before hanging up. Then I went in search of vitamin E. Too bad Charlie didn't tell me the stuff was sticky and yucky.

On the way to the kitchen I caught a glimpse of myself in the mirror. Big mistake. I made Quasimodo look as if he'd stepped off the pages of *GQ*.

"Oh, my," Mama said when she saw me. She'd always been great at understatement.

"Don't say it. I used sunblock. I obviously didn't slather on enough." I gulped half a glass of orange juice.

"And what is *this* stuff?" She lightly fingered the gunk on my arm.

"Vitamin E. Charlie claims it's good for sunburn."

"Oh." When Mama lapsed into the "oh" mode, it usually didn't bode well for the next topic of conversation.

"You're spending a lot of your vacation

with that Morrison boy." She glanced in a meaningful way at my ring.

"Mama! The man's a doctor, so I hardly believe he qualifies as *that Morrison boy* anymore."

Mama looked as if she was about to respond, but instead rummaged through the refrigerator. "You're right. His name is Charlie. Now, would you like eggs or pancakes?"

"Orange juice is fine for now, thanks. If I get hungry I'll fix some toast."

"Oh." There it was again.

"Mama, you want to say something, so just tell me."

She seemed hesitant. That was not typical of my assertive mother.

"I've wanted to tell you this for a while. Your daddy and I made a mistake about Charlie. I'm afraid all those years ago we didn't give him the benefit of the doubt."

No kidding!

"So I'd like you to invite him to dinner. We want to make amends. Your daddy would like to apologize."

Talk about being blown away! I was left

speechless. What had Daddy done back in 1973? I was about to ask when the phone rang.

"Yes, she's here. I'll put her on." Mama paused, listening to someone on the other end of the line. "Nice talking to you, too."

"It's Professor Rinaldi," she said, handing me the phone. Mama had never been very enthusiastic about either of the Rinaldi men. When Dom and I announced our engagement, my parents' response was tepid at best.

"Hi, Santo. How are you feeling?"

"I'm at home and that makes me happy. I'm going in tomorrow for more tests, but do not worry, *bambina,* everything will be fine. I'm calling to see if you're having fun."

"I am," I said, although to be completely honest this conversation was giving me a guilty twinge. "Will Dom be able to go to the doctor with you?" It was pitiful that I didn't have any idea what my fiancé was doing.

"Oh, no, no. That's not necessary. He's still in Costa Rica."

My guilt pangs increased in intensity. The

minute I got off the phone with Santo, I started tracking down his son. I had to find out what was happening, because I had a *bad* feeling.

It took me a while, but I eventually caught Dom in his hotel room. "How's Costa Rica?" I decided to keep him in a good mood by asking about work.

"Fantastic," he said, launching into a monologue concerning the project.

I listened to him with half an ear and added a few appropriate remarks. When he finally wound down, I asked, "What's going on with your dad?"

His pause only served to heighten my anxiety. "He has to go in for further tests. I don't know what they're looking for, and Dad's being closemouthed."

"Don't you think one of us should be there?"

"No, I don't. He'll be mad if we cut our trips short."

"Are you sure?"

"I'm positive."

I wasn't certain I believed him, but Santo was his father, not mine—not really.

couldn't begin to imagine what they'd done; whatever it was must've been bad.

Mama was a much better cook than I was, so my contribution to our lovely dinner was grunt work—peeling sweet potatoes, washing lettuce and so forth.

It wasn't until we'd gorged on the best of a Southern mama's cooking and moved out to the patio for coffee that my intuition kicked in. Something big was about to occur. I couldn't tell whether it was good, hideous or somewhere in between.

"Charlie." Daddy began to speak and then halted, looking distinctly uncomfortable. My daddy was the most confident man in the world and he was rendered speechless. Uh-oh! This was a man who'd spent most of his adult life with a big gun strapped to his hip.

"I'd like to apologize for what happened when you kids were in high school," he said solemnly.

Charlie looked as surprised by my dad's comment as I was. In fact, he appeared dumbstruck.

"Um." After a few minutes Charlie grinned. "Well, sir. I accept your apology."

I tried to ask what that was all about, but Charlie stopped me by squeezing my hand.

"Let's go for a boat ride," he suggested.

Instead of driving to our house, Charlie had motored over in one of his parents' powerboats.

"Okay." What else could I say when he was pulling me to my feet?

"Thank you, sir. I realize that wasn't easy, and I want you to know I appreciate it." He shook Daddy's hand, eliciting smiles from both of my parents. "Now, if you folks don't mind, I'd like to take Jazzy for a moonlight cruise."

"You kids have fun." Daddy looked like a teenager as he took Mama's hand. Apparently they didn't take my engagement all that seriously—which was interesting to say the least. "We old folks are going to sit here and enjoy the evening."

Charlie and I strolled to the dock, where he helped me into the boat. Dusk had changed to dark, highlighting the soothing sounds of a summer night. No matter where

I was or what I was doing, when the calendar turned to summer, I always had a longing for this part of Texas.

Patience had never been my forte; however, I managed to wait until we were well away from the house before I pressed Charlie for answers.

"What was going on back there?" It was difficult to talk over the motor's noise, but my curiosity was killing me.

Charlie pushed my hair behind my ear and placed a string of kisses from my chin to the tender spot at the base of my ear.

"Let's dock and then we can have a long chat." He drew into a cove that was our favorite swimming spot all through elementary and junior high school.

Charlie tied the boat to an old wharf. Watching the movement of muscles beneath his polo shirt led to ideas I shouldn't be having. I twisted the ring on my left hand. Nope, jumping his bones was out of the question.

"Let's sit in the back of the boat and get comfortable." He took my hand and urged me toward the cushions at the rear of the vessel. "I was hoping we'd have a chance to talk. So, being an optimist I brought some drinks." He removed a cooler from under the seat. "Could I interest you in some wine?" Charlie pulled out a bottle of chilled chardonnay.

I laughed. "Does this topic require alcohol?"

Charlie winked in response. "Yep, I suspect it might. This isn't exactly what I was planning to discuss, but I'm flexible. You want to know what your dad was talking about, right?"

"Damned straight I do."

"You remember the summer of our senior year."

Considering it had colored the rest of my future, yeah, I remembered it. "Uh-huh."

"And you remember how it ended."

Talk about an event that was indelibly imprinted on my memory. "Oh, yeah!"

"I owe you an apology for how I acted. But—" he paused "—I was a scared kid."

"Scared of what?"

"More of a who than a what. Your dad

made it quite clear that I had to stay away from you. He scared the crap out of me."

Did I really hear that? Surely he couldn't mean my father had threatened him. I'd assumed my dad had a hand in manipulating the situation, but threaten Charlie? No way, no how!

"What did he say?" I had to ask, even though I wasn't sure I wanted to hear the answer.

"His warning was vague, but his meaning was clear. In a nutshell, he said I'd be toast if I didn't leave you alone. I'm fairly certain he knew you were thinking about changing schools and he was afraid I'd interfere with your future. Your parents really thought you should go to Berkeley. I *know* they had your best interests at heart."

His answer astonished me. It also explained why Charlie had done such an about-face on our relationship. He'd been shunned by the rest of the community, so how could he expect a fair deal if my dad went after him? Not that in my wildest dreams did I think Daddy really would have followed through with his threat. Charlie had believed it, though.

"I'm so sorry."

"That's okay. It was a long time ago."

Then something else occurred to me. "How did you know I was considering UT?" I was almost positive I hadn't let him in on my secret.

"Misty told me."

All I could do was shake my head. With friends like that, who needed enemies?

"I'm sure she didn't tell my dad," I said with certainty.

"No, I don't think so, either. But you know how accurate the Meadow Lake grapevine is. Someone from the post office probably mentioned it."

"Oh, my Lord."

"That's why I live in Denver." On the surface, he was discussing the audacity of the rumor mill. However, I could tell he was also talking about how screwed up that summer had been.

"Don't be too hard on your parents. They were trying to do what was best for you."

I wanted to pitch a hissy—a humongous,

big, fat hissy fit. But what would that accomplish other than to elevate my blood pressure?

"I can't believe this." I dropped my head into my hands to ruminate for a few minutes. Since I'd decided to forgo the tantrum, I at least deserved to have a good old-fashioned teeth-gnashing. When I finally glanced up, Charlie was handing me a glass of wine. He was also wearing one of his silly grins.

A girl would have to be dead to resist that man's charm, and I certainly wasn't dead. Au contraire! I was alive and itching for some action of the Charlie variety. I was in big trouble.

"Jazzy," he said as he took the plastic glass from my hand, "I need you." Charlie cupped my chin and slowly lowered his mouth to mine.

It started out like a glorious homecoming—warm, inviting and comfortable—but when he deepened the kiss I was a goner. I was seventeen all over again, and experiencing the thrill of first love. Everything except Charlie ceased to exist. At that moment he was the center of this universe; he'd become the epicenter of my reality. I wanted to climb into his skin with him.

Holy tamoley!

I belonged with Charlie; that was clear to me. And that meant I had to call off my engagement to Dom.

Charlie ran his fingers through my hair, slowly twisting the strands. It took every molecule of restraint to keep from whimpering. I wanted to moan and sigh, but that would've been *so* soap opera. Who would've suspected that a hundred-dollar haircut could harbor a secondary erogenous zone?

In moments of lucidity, my pesky inner voice kept repeating that mantra of "remember Dom" and "you're still engaged." To which I mentally uttered "Dom who?" and twisted the diamond to the inside of my hand. That, of course, was putting *out of sight, out of mind* to the ultimate test.

It worked, sort of, as we delved into a mad foray of tongues and lips and teeth. I barely had a second to come up for a breath, and that was only when I remembered to breathe.

Charlie lifted his head and stared at me with those beautiful sea-foam-green eyes. "I want you so bad I ache." He leaned his forehead against mine. "I've never stopped thinking about you."

That made two of us. With a blinding sense of clarity, I realized I'd made a horrific mistake by not trying to find out what went wrong that summer, so many years ago. I also knew that before this went any further, I had to make some hard decisions about Dom. Decisions that, for all intents and purposes, I'd already made.

"Oh, Charlie, Charlie, Charlie." This time I couldn't repress the sigh. "I've thought about you, too. So often I've wondered what you were doing and how things could've worked out for us. But right now's not a good time for me." I held up my hand and the ring twinkled in the moonlight, emphasizing the fact that I was engaged—for the moment, anyway.

I didn't have any idea what his intentions were, but I plunged ahead. "I have to straighten out my life before I can even think about us."

My epiphany had also included the realization that I didn't love Dom the way I should. I'd always had a sneaking suspicion that there was something missing in our relationship, and this thing with Charlie confirmed my misgivings.

Charlie kissed me gently and pulled me into a hug that was warm and comforting. "Okay, for now. But I'll give you fair warning—this is not over."

I sure hoped not.

He picked up my wineglass and refilled it. "Let's talk. You can tell me everything you've done in the past twenty years."

And I did. We laughed and talked and laughed some more. The birds had started chirping, announcing the break of dawn, when we decided to call it a night.

I was happier than I'd been in a *very* long time.

Chapter 20

Through the thick fugue of sleep, I heard a noise. Uh-oh. It was the William Tell Overture. What had possessed me to choose that ring tone? And what idiot would call me at…good heavens, it was eleven o'clock. The sun was shining, the birds were singing, the world was functioning, and I was still wallowing in bed. Who wouldn't be after falling asleep at 6:00 a.m.?

"Hello," I croaked.

"Jazzy, is that you?"

"Whatcha need, Mary Alice?"

"Did I wake you?" she asked. "I'm sorry."

Only Mary Alice would apologize for an almost-noon phone call.

"No, no. I'm just a little congested."

"Oh…" She paused. "You're never going to believe this." This pause was more significant than the last one.

"What?"

"Bunny's here."

Now it was my turn to go silent. Damn! And double damn! "She's here?"

"Yep, she just called me. Can you believe it?"

Oh, I could believe it. I could feel in my bones that my luck was about to go south.

"What's she doing here?" That was a dumb question.

Mary Alice obviously thought it was stupid, too. "She's in town for the reunion?" Her voice rose up at the end of the sentence, rendering it a question for the not-so-bright.

"She wants all of us to get together for drinks this afternoon, at her parents' place."

A Brazilian bikini wax sounded more appealing than going to the Bennetts' mansion for drinks. "Who's *all* of us?" Please God, she wasn't inviting Charlie to this soiree.

"You, me, Petey, Charlie and Bill. Misty's still in Austin. It'll just be the old gang. We'll have a great time."

That was a matter of opinion. With everything else I had swirling around in my head, I wasn't ready for a Bunny encounter. Especially not the way I was feeling about Charlie.

We talked for a few moments before Mary Alice said she had a customer. The minute we disconnected I threw myself back into bed and pulled the pillow over my face. This was not going to be a good day; I could feel impending doom right down to the tips of my toes.

The next call was from Charlie. "Did you hear?" That was all he said. He didn't have to elaborate.

"Uh-huh."

"Are you going?"

"I guess. Mary Alice would have my scalp if I didn't."

"Then I'm picking you up. I've always figured there's safety in numbers."

I wasn't sure any scenario involving

Bunny would be safe, but if Charlie was with me I could keep an eye on him.

"Okay. What time?"

"M.A. said to be there around five. So I'll pick you up at about four-thirty."

Whoopee, I couldn't wait. Although Bunny had been a good friend in high school, it was years since I'd heard from her. And so much had happened.... This evening couldn't be anything but painful— very painful.

I stumbled out of bed and made my way to the caffeine. Thank goodness the pot was full of hot, aromatic coffee.

After I made it back to the land of the living, I dug through my closet trying to find the ideal outfit. My search revealed I hadn't packed anything resembling the perfect outfit; in fact, I wasn't sure I even *owned* the perfect outfit. Where was that sexy little sundress when I needed it?

It was at Mary Alice's store, that's where. No time like the present for some quality shopping. I hopped into my Saturn rental and buzzed into town. Little did I know this was only the first of many shopping expeditions I'd make to Mary Alice's Boutique. My wardrobe was pitiful.

"Hey, Jazzy. I'm so glad you came by," Mary Alice squealed.

"I need to buy something to wear tonight. Then I thought we could go for coffee."

"That's terrific. I have just the thing." She scurried out from behind the counter and riffled through a rack of brightly colored dresses. My entire wardrobe consisted of business suits, so whatever she chose would be a huge style change.

"Ta-da! Here it is." She held up a red dress that could barely be classified as a dress, or a scrap, or anything else that resembled clothing. It was short, really short. Plus it was a halter.

"Uh, where's the back on this thing?" I turned the hanger around, hoping more fabric would magically appear.

"Don't be a prude. You'll look *great* in it. I'm sure it's the right size." Mary Alice pushed me toward the dressing room. "I'll keep looking in case that one doesn't work."

As I slipped on the little nothing, I realized she was right. It was fantastic. Not much to it, but eye-popping nevertheless. And if I was even vaguely correct about Charlie's intentions, he'd bust a gut when he saw me. I twirled in front of the mirror and hoped to goodness I wasn't kidding myself. This whole experience was making me feel like I was seventeen again.

"What do you think?" I asked as I came out of the dressing room. Predictably, Mary Alice squealed.

"That's, oh, wow! That's fantastic."

"Should I keep searching?" Not that I really planned to pass this one up, but I couldn't resist making her squeal.

"No!" M.A. didn't disappoint me.

"So help me find something for that stupid prom on Saturday. I have a feeling the dress I brought won't do at all."

Ever the saleswoman, Mary Alice plastered on a grin and pulled out dress after dress. I vetoed most of them, but I eventually decided to try on a white slinky number and a black dress that was missing most of the front. What was with designers skimping on material?

Fortunately, or unfortunately, the white one fit like a dream, and the very, very low-cut cowl neck covered all the essentials.

"The black's really nice but that white one—ooh-la-la," M.A. declared.

She had me convinced until I noticed that the price tag contained more numbers than my monthly car payment.

I made a final twirl in front of the mirror and darn it all, I really did like what I saw. Even my butt looked good.

"Okay, I'll take the red sundress and this one. Is it too early to go for a glass of wine?"

"How about a margarita? You can't beat Alberto's. They make terrific nachos, too."

That suggestion was too hard to resist.

Charlie was appreciative, and that was a reaction I wasn't used to, especially from Dom. A wardrobe update *was* in order.

"You're gorgeous," he said, giving me a thorough inspection. "Absolutely fantastic!" I was tempted to buy a closetful of hot red dresses.

"Are you ready?" he asked.

I guess that all depended on what he

wanted me to be ready for. Oh, right—the party. I had to keep focused.

"Ready as I'll ever be," I answered, grabbing the tiny purse Mary Alice had insisted would complete the outfit. She said my clunky shoulder bag was too gauche for words.

After we turned onto the highway, I had to ask the question that had been bugging me all day. "What do you think about Bunny being home?"

Charlie glanced at me and shrugged. "Doesn't make much difference. I'm still mad about the way she treated me that last summer, but I guess it doesn't really matter anymore. It's all in the past."

Much as I hated to admit it, I was still mad at her, too. She'd ditched all of us without a backward look, and now she was strolling home as if nothing had ever happened.

The Bennetts' mansion hadn't changed much in the past twenty years. Although subdivisions were encroaching, the palatial grounds reminded me of a castle moat. Instead of a water-filled ditch they used acres and acres of immaculately groomed St. Augustine grass to discourage unwanted visitors.

"I've always hated this place," I admitted as we drove into the circular driveway.

Charlie flashed me one of his wry grins. "You don't know the half of it. The first time I picked Bunny up for a date, I was afraid I was going to get frisked or shot. I should've taken it as a bad omen. After that, we met on the sly."

"Yeah."

He pulled up next to Mary Alice's minivan and cut the engine. "Shall we go in?"

Before I could answer, he pulled me across the console and kissed me thoroughly. Whew! *Now* I was ready, although we looked like we'd been in a lipstick-smearing contest. I retrieved a tissue from my purse and dabbed his face. Now I had to repair my carefully applied makeup. It wouldn't do to show up looking like we'd had a hot and heavy make-out session—even though that was exactly what we'd been doing, and enjoying every minute of it.

"Is my dress okay?" Enough of that. I was

a successful, professional woman, but somehow those pubescent doubts lingered on.

"Fabulous. And so are you." Charlie punctuated his comment with a kiss to the sensitive side of my neck. Talk about goosebump city.

When Charlie pushed the doorbell, chimes like Big Ben reverberated throughout the old mansion. I was deliberating on all things ostentatious when a gorgeous blonde answered the door. She'd been coiffed and coutured by the best New York had to offer. She was also wearing a diamond the size of a small pigeon's egg. Lordy, that bauble made my rock look like something out of a Cracker Jack box.

"Jazzy, I didn't expect you to come with Charlie." Before I could make a suitable comment, Bunny air-kissed me, then turned her attention to Charlie.

"And Charlie, you're certainly looking handsome."

Good grief! Bunny was checking him out as if he were a thick steak and she was ready to chow down.

Mary Alice and Petey were standing behind her, obviously uncomfortable. Sure as shootin', this was a debacle in the making.

The longer I stayed in Meadow Lake, the more Texas my thoughts and accent became.

"Come on in and I'll get you a drink." Bunny took Charlie's arm, leaving me standing on the front porch like an unwanted salesman.

"Get in here," Mary Alice demanded as she jerked me into the foyer. "What did you do, make a detour through Houston?"

"What?" We were about ten minutes late. Why was she making a federal case out of that?

"She's already made a pass at Petey *and* Bill."

I stopped dead in my tracks. "Petey?" I asked with some measure of incredulity.

Mary Alice wrinkled her nose and gave me a truly magnificent drop-dead look. "Yes. Petey."

The man in question grinned. Even though it was sickly, it was a smile. Sort of. I didn't want to know what Bill's response had been; something profane, I was sure. He'd never been a member of Bunny's fan club. It probably had to do with the fact that she'd blackmailed him on more than one occasion.

"Anyone else here?" Although a number of cars were parked in the driveway, for all I knew they belonged to the Bennetts.

"There are about ten people out by the pool. You should recognize them. Most are members of the reunion committee."

Bunny and Charlie were at the bar by the time we reached the patio. I was well on my way to the pissed-off stage. Charlie was *my* date. Wasn't he?

Instead of obsessing, I decided to check out my old classmates. Mary Alice was right about one thing; there was a crowd around the pool. She was wrong in her contention that I'd recognize any of them. I didn't see a familiar face in the group except for Bill, and he wasn't a happy camper.

More than likely he'd accepted the invitation because he assumed Misty would be there. Poor man—Misty wouldn't spit on him if he were going off like a Roman candle.

To Charlie's credit, he appeared to be trying to get out of Bunny's clutches.

"What's she doing?" I asked Mary Alice, not that I really expected an answer.

I trusted Charlie, honestly I did. Bunny was another story, though—especially in her newest incarnation. Even as gorgeously turned out as she was, there was an air about her that made me want to hum the tune from *Jaws*.

In a vain attempt to smooth the waters and avert a scene, Mary Alice towed me over to greet some folks I wouldn't have known if I'd slammed into them with my shopping cart. Actually—and shame on me—there were some I couldn't place even *after* I heard their names. Fortunately I was adept at the cocktail party tap dance.

The entire time I was doing the "how's your mama" routine, I was secretly spying on Charlie and Bunny. They appeared to be immersed in a serious conversation. Bunny's hands were waving up and down; she was either attempting to make a point, or trying to get her way about something.

I briefly considered smacking our hostess, and then it hit me. I was jealous. Whole-heartedly, mind-numbingly jealous. Oh, boy, that confirmed what I already suspected. I was in love with Charlie!

To be completely honest, I'd never been *out* of love with him. Despite the years, I still loved him like I did back in high school.

That was a huge problem. It meant I had to do something drastic about Dom, like breaking up with him. And that was assuming Charlie was still interested.

No time like the present to determine his stand on the issue. Chin up, chest out (or as far out as a good A cup could go), and plaster on a big smile. Now I was ready to take on the enemy, or in this case, my old friend.

"Hi, Bunny." I was trying to be oh, so gracious. As much as I wanted to blame her for our estrangement, it wasn't all her fault. When I was living in California, I'd intended to write her but never did. "How have you been?" I asked.

"Fantastic," Bunny gushed. She sounded as if she'd be at home at a polo match in the Hamptons. "Absolutely fantastic."

Was this the same person who was born

and raised in south Texas? To hear her talk, you'd never know chicken-fried steak used to be her favorite food.

"I understand you live in New York City." It wasn't the most scintillating comment in the world, but she wasn't exactly holding up her end of the exchange. Maybe her exclusive girls' school hadn't offered Conversation 101.

Miraculously Charlie escaped her grip and sidled up next to me.

"We have an apartment in Manhattan, but I spend most of my time at our home in Amagansett."

Did I nail that one or what? Bunny was a quintessential Hamptons matron.

"Really?" Before I could complete my sentence, she strolled off, although wiggled would be a better description.

"What were you two talking about?" I asked.

"I'm not sure," Charlie said, cupping my elbow and steering me to the bar. "Let's get a drink and find a quiet place to sit."

Although that sounded a bit ominous, I followed him as if he were the Pied Piper.

We filled our glasses and Charlie found a couple of chairs away from the crowd. As I said before, patience was not one of my long suits—just ask my parents. However, I managed to contain my natural edginess. Somehow I kept quiet while Charlie studied his shoes, the flagstone patio, the stars and just about everything around us but my face.

"Bunny was telling me she had a miscarriage shortly after she left town."

By the time he finally spoke, I'd leaned back in the chaise and closed my eyes.

"Did you tell her you already knew?"

"No. I felt it was her story to share."

"Perhaps. But think of it this way—everything she and her family did affected us. So is it really her story?" I didn't bother to add that during the past two decades many of my personal decisions had been colored by the events of that summer.

And darn it, Bunny was back in the picture!

Chapter 21

After a long, sleepless night, I decided to end my engagement immediately. I didn't love Dom the way you should love someone you're planning to marry. So to be fair to both of us, I was going to give him back his ring. My decision had huge implications.

I'd always subscribed to the theory that when confronted with an unpleasant task, gut up and do it. So before I lost my nerve, I picked up my cell and punched in Dom's number.

He picked up on the third ring. "Hi, Dom. Are you back in California?"

I could hear paper rustling in the background, so I knew he was distracted. "I've been here a day. What do you need?"

No *I love you,* no *I miss you,* nothing personal, just *What do you need?*

"Dom, I want your full attention."

He was silent for a moment. "Jasmine, is there a problem?"

Yep, there *was* a problem. "Um, I think... um, I think I should do this in person, but I...um, I..."

"Jasmine," he said with great patience. "What are you trying to tell me?"

"I'm returning your ring. We're not getting married," I blurted, instantly regretting my lack of tact.

There was a long pause on his end of the line. "What?"

"We're not getting married."

"You can't be serious."

"I am so sorry. I've known this was coming for a long time, but I tried to ignore it."

Dom was being unusually curt. "We'll talk about it when you get home."

"No, I'm not going to change my mind. But we can discuss it after we've both had a chance to do some thinking. I realize it's a shock, but after you've thought about it, you'll understand."

"You're wrong. I'm going to hang up." The next sound I heard was a dial tone. Whoa! That didn't go well.

He didn't believe me, and I knew I couldn't convince him over the phone. I wasn't even positive I could do it in person. When it suited him, he could be very stubborn. None of that mattered, though; I was sure of what I wanted. With that in mind, I took off the ring and stowed it in my old jewelry box.

I was still pondering my "bull in the china shop" routine when my phone rang again. Assuming it was Dom, I answered with trepidation.

Instead, the voice on the other end of the line belonged to Patty Perky, aka Mary Alice. "Are you ready?" She was talking about the impending "prom" disaster. I had more important fish to fry—like my situation with Dom and my Bunny encounter— but Mary Alice wasn't responsible for either problem.

"As ready as I'll ever be," I answered. After last night I wasn't too sure about anything, other than Charlie.

"Five o'clock at our house for cocktails," M.A. ordered. She was being bossy again.

"Five o'clock. Yes, ma'am."

"And bring Charlie," she said in her best sergeant-major voice.

"I'll remind him." But I knew he hadn't forgotten.

"Hi, Charlie." I sounded like the California version of Perky Patty. "Mary Alice asked me to jog your memory about being invited to their house for drinks prior to the prom."

"I remember."

Oops, he was being terse. "Do you still want to go?"

There was silence and then a sigh. "My partners in Denver are taking care of my patients so I can be here. I'm not going to let Bunny ruin this for us. I'll pick you up around four-thirty."

His voice dropped to an intimate caress.

"Did I tell you how terrific you looked last night?"

Charlie's slow honeyed drawl almost gave me the vapors—whatever vapors might be. "Uh-huh."

"I can't wait to see you."

"Uh-huh." Had I really graduated cum laude? If that was true, why wasn't I more articulate? Lust—that's what it was. It was seeping through every one of my pores. That and the fact that I'd finally decided to follow my heart.

I wasn't disappointed by Charlie's reaction to my new image. Being sexy was fun! Goodwill was about to get a bundle of black, blue and taupe suits. Red was the hallmark of my new image.

Charlie handed me a bouquet of daisies and yellow roses. "I couldn't go the corsage route," he admitted. "So, I hoped you'd like these."

"I love them." I sniffed the flowers. "They're perfect."

Mama and Daddy joined us in the hall. Swear to goodness, I half expected them to pull out a camera. It felt as if I'd stepped into a remake of *Back to the Future*.

"Have a good time," Mama said, kissing me on the cheek.

She was matchmaking! That was certainly a case of doing over the past. I wondered if she noticed my ring was missing. Charlie obviously did because he was caressing the fingers of my left hand. A long, serious talk was in our future.

I wasn't sure who I should expect at Mary Alice's house. To my immense relief, the gathering was restricted to the four of us. M.A. was stressed to the max and even Petey looked like he was about to crash and burn.

"The DJ just called and said he had a wreck and his equipment's spread all over the freeway," she wailed.

Uh, oh—what was a prom without music? I hid my secret smile. This would be a great excuse to cancel, wouldn't it?

"I phoned everyone I could think of and came up with a big, fat zip. Nada. Nothing."

This time Mary Alice's voice broke as if

she was on the verge of lapsing into a full-blown frenzy. Oh, please. Not that.

"Sweetie pie, don't worry. We'll figure something out, won't we, Jazzy?" Petey said, trying to comfort his wife.

He gave me a look that sent a shudder right down to the tips of my toes. Darn him, he'd perfected that hangdog expression in high school and he apparently still used it.

"Um, I guess." What did I know about the south Texas music scene? "Petey, you're bound to have some band connections. Maybe the kids at school know someone who can help." It was a long shot, but I was fresh out of suggestions.

Petey didn't seem inclined to ask a teenager for a favor; however, he dutifully headed over to the phone. Love like that was hard to find.

"Mary Alice, everything will be fine. I'm sure of it." I wasn't sure of anything, much less the possibility that someone would want to provide music for a bunch of middle-aged prom-goers. This whole idea was a disaster in the making.

Charlie opened the wine and was plying

Mary Alice with booze. I wasn't convinced that would work, but any port in a storm, so to speak. If memory served me right, Mary Alice didn't lose her cool very often, but when she did, everyone dived for cover.

In the background I could hear Petey muttering on the phone. The only distinct word I heard was "crap."

That wasn't a positive omen.

By the time Petey finally worked a miracle, Charlie had refilled Mary Alice's glass not once, not twice, but thrice.

"Okay, here's the deal. We have two options. I found a DJ who can work tonight."

Mary Alice's face brightened, that is until Petey continued his explanation.

"But…" He paused and bit his lip. "He does *gangsta* rap."

"What?" she screeched. "Did you say *gangsta* rap?"

"Uh-huh," Petey muttered, sliding his arms around his wife. "The good news is he thinks he can come up with old copies of the 'Electric Slide' and 'YMCA.' Hey, sweetie." He put a finger under her chin, forcing her to meet his eyes. "We don't have many choices. It's either use this DJ or—the other option—borrow a boom box."

I could see the wheels turning in her brain as she came to grips with his logic.

"Okay." She sniffed and then reverted to her typical Mary Alice personality. "It could be fun. No! This *will* be fun."

Charlie and I glanced at each other, his face mirroring my doubt.

Fun? No way. Fiasco? Oh, yeah.

The Moose Lodge was awash in a sea of balloons and crepe paper. Some enterprising soul had even managed to find a glittery disco ball. John Travolta, eat your heart out.

Charlie was apparently experiencing the same retro déjà vu I was. "Can you believe this?" he whispered. His lips were tantalizingly close, eliciting lascivious ideas and memories of warm summer nights and hot, hot lovin'.

Yikes! What was *that* all about? Oh, right, he was the star player in every one of my erotic fantasies. I could feel the flush rise up my neck. Did a person ever get too old to blush?

Charlie stared at me. "Are you hot?"

"Um, no, why do you ask?" I could brazen this out.

"You seem kind of pink."

No kidding! Two decades of prurient thoughts had just raced through my head.

"Would you like to have Dr. Morrison examine you?" he offered, flashing me a suggestive grin.

Would I ever!

"Let's go to the bar," he said.

I nodded in agreement, hoping they stocked something more exotic than chardonnay out of a cardboard box.

As much as I'd dreaded this get-together, I had to admit it had the potential to be entertaining. Not that I was a snob, but wow, some of the outfits were a wee bit hard to believe.

Charlie handed me a plastic glass of wine. "Here you go, Sunshine."

I hated to sound ungrateful and, regardless of its origin, I planned to drink it, but I had to ask. "Did this come out of a box?"

He gave me one of *those* grins. "Nope, he poured it out of a bottle. I promise. Did you see Buster Smith's duds?" Charlie pointed at a portly guy in a turquoise tuxedo.

"That's Buster Smith?" I remembered Buster as a scrawny predecessor to the computer geek, complete with a pocket protector and a slide rule. The high-school version wouldn't have been caught dead in *that* outrageous getup.

"Yep, that's Buster. I wouldn't have recognized him if he hadn't introduced himself. The woman in the matching dress is his wife. They own an insurance agency here in town."

I was trying to keep my eyes from popping out when Misty strolled up with Bill in tow. Although Misty would deny it with her dying breath, the sexual tension between those two was intense.

"You're gorgeous," Misty said as she hugged me. "So are you," she told Charlie with a wink.

"Ditto to you," I told her. Jeez, we sounded like a mutual admiration society, but she did look fantastic in an unadorned black minisheath, her bright red hair loose and unrestrained.

"Did you guys come together?" I asked. She hadn't told me she had a date, but they certainly were chummy.

"No. He followed me in. Uninvited, I might add." Her eloquent snort punctuated her obvious disapproval.

Oops—wrong question! I was wondering how to begin again when Charlie saved the day. "Hey, guy." He clapped a hand on Bill's shoulder. "Let's go over to the bar and see about getting you a drink."

I waited until they'd walked off before I gave in to my curiosity. "What's going on?"

Misty shrugged sheepishly. I suspected that my district attorney friend was accustomed to charging in with guns blazing. Hesitancy had to be new for her.

"We've been talking on the phone. A lot." She glanced around as if trying to determine whether anyone was listening. "His DEA office is in downtown Austin, so we've been meeting for lunch, too."

"And?"

"And," she grimaced. "I think he's incredibly sexy. And nice."

"Join the crowd. Who would've suspected

Billy Tom, of all people, would grow up to look like that?" I waved toward the bar where Charlie and Bill were yukking it up with a couple of other guys, as yet to be identified.

Man, I hated the fact that I had to have a name tag to recognize anyone.

"He goes by Bill," she said, returning a smile.

I looked from Misty to Bill, and back to Misty again. "Then why are you being so tacky to him?"

"I don't know. I guess I'm just bitchy."

No kidding. "If you want to keep going to lunch with him, you'd be a lot smarter to use the honey routine."

Misty thought about my suggestion. "You're probably right. I have this—" she made apostrophes in the air "—*thing* about getting serious with a guy. It's colored every relationship I've tried."

Misty had confided in me that she was date-raped while she was in law school, but I'd been so involved with my own life and career I hadn't made sure she was okay. Now, I had to assume that although she'd had extensive therapy, her recovery wasn't complete.

"You remember what I told you about the rape?"

We were about to tread on very sensitive territory. "Yes."

"Several years back, the same guy tracked me down and started stalking me. I refused to feel that vulnerable again, so I pressed charges against him. That's when I became interested in prosecuting sexual offenders and joined the District Attorney's office."

"Oh, Misty. I didn't know."

"I only told you so you'd understand where I'm coming from."

"Bill's a nice guy. He won't hurt you. Remember the time he took us to the drive-in to get drunk?"

Misty giggled at the memory. "I remember it like it was yesterday. I had such a crush on Bucky, and there I was puking petals."

We both laughed recalling that ignominious scene.

"You're right. Bill's a good man. I'll drag out my best party manners. I promise," Misty conceded. "Let's round up the boys and find a place to sit. We'll save Mary Alice and Petey a spot, although I'm not sure M.A. will actually sit down."

About that time Mary Alice flitted by. "Did you hear the DJ is a no-show and his replacement specializes in *gangsta* rap?" she asked.

"No way!" Misty squealed.

I hoped squealing wasn't contagious.

"Way!"

That sent us both into a spell of giggling. It felt great to be able to laugh with old friends.

"The guys are staring," I commented. "They think we're talking about them."

"Uh-huh," Misty agreed. "Curiosity is good. It puts them on edge. Don't tell anyone, but it's a tactic I use when I have a witness on the stand," she confided as she pranced to the bar.

A barbecue buffet was the choice of cuisine, and what better culinary delight to serve at a south Texas high-school reunion? A sniff of mesquite smoke and sizzling meat made my taste buds sit up and salute—but tuxes and brisket?

Wasn't that a bit of a stretch?

"You might consider using your napkin like a lobster bib," Misty said, accompanying her comment with an irritating smile.

Damn! She remembered my proclivity for stains. Back in high school, Misty claimed you could figure out the cafeteria menu by checking my blouse. Sheesh—I'd outgrown that, hadn't I?

I glanced at my pristine white, very expensive dress and cringed, imagining a big glop of dark brown sauce smack-dab in the middle.

"Smart mouth." That was a mild version of what I really wanted to say. "I've dined at some of the most exclusive restaurants in the Bay Area without embarrassing myself." I wasn't planning to have a klutz relapse—not here and not now.

Charlie squeezed my knee and winked. "When did you perfect that prissy tone?" In a much lower voice he said, "I have to say it turned me on. Maybe later I can convince you to play one of my favorite games. It's called the countess and the gardener."

My eyes must've been the size of dinner plates. Dom wasn't quirky and lighthearted; *serious* was more his style. But much to my delight, Charlie had never lost his sense of fun.

"A countess?" I muttered. I was a smart girl, so why couldn't I come up with some brilliant quip?

Charlie kissed the side of my neck and whispered, "Don't knock it till you've tried it. Trust me, you'll love it." He emphasized his assertion with a nibble on my earlobe and a grin. Yep, it was the same smile that turned my knees to jelly and my brain to mush. A girl would have to be dead not to respond to Charlie's charm, and I was far from dead.

"I do trust you," I said, and it was true. That was a darned good thing because I was about to trust my heart to him.

"There's one stipulation," I added. "When I play the countess, you have to grant my every wish." I might be a slow learner in the art of sexual innuendo, but by gosh I was about to get the hang of it. I only hoped I wouldn't resort to fluttering my eyelashes.

That would be *so* junior high!

Before Charlie could do anything more than smirk, Bunny made a grand entrance. And what an entrance it was! My expertise when it came to couture fashions was practically nonexistent, but even *I* could tell her outfit cost more than my house payment. And considering I lived in the Bay Area, my mortgage was nothing to sneeze at.

"Did you save this place for little old me?" she drawled. All traces of Bunny's Long Island accent were gone. Undoubtedly that was due to an excess of Jack Daniel's. Oh, dear. This situation had the potential to go bad—fast.

"Certainly." Misty started to assure our friend that we intended to include her— until Bunny draped herself all over Bill.

"Mmm." She ran a hand suggestively down Bill's chest, popping buttons along the way. "How did you grow up to be such a sexy man?" That wouldn't have been so bad, but then she decided to check out his tonsils.

Misty was going to kill her. Kill her dead!

"Do something," I whispered to Charlie. Watching a slow-motion wreck was not my idea of a good time—and this one was going to be a fifteen-car pileup.

Charlie, bless his heart, jumped into action. "Hey, Misty, dance with me." He didn't give her a chance to say no before he hauled her to her feet.

"I don't know how to dance to that stuff," Misty complained.

Charlie made a comic shimmy. "Let's give it a shot. We couldn't be any worse than those two." He indicated Mr. and Mrs. Buster Smith, who'd launched into dirty dancing. Imagine that.

There was a lot to love about a man who didn't mind making a fool of himself in the name of friendship.

"Oh, all right." Misty threw her napkin on the table. "You—" she pointed a crimson nail at Bill "—behave."

"Yes, ma'am." He immediately jettisoned Bunny from his lap.

Great, just great. Mary Alice and Petey were missing in action, Misty was attacking the dance floor like she was prosecuting a serial killer and Bill had made a mad dash to the bar. It was up to me to corral our friend.

"Bunny, why don't we go to the ladies' room?"

"Excellent idea." Her giggle at the end of the sentence should've been a huge warning, but I must not have been listening.

The minute we hit the bathroom, Bunny made a beeline for a stall. Wait a minute! This humanitarian mission was looking more and more like an unwelcome replay of college. I'd had this suite mate… Oh, never mind. At any rate, Bunny ended up worshipping the porcelain god and I was grossed out. She was *not* an attractive drunk.

"Oh, no," she wailed, sinking back on her heels. "Oh, crap!"

Half my brain urged me to let her embarrass herself; the other half said, *hey, she's an old friend.* Oops! Someone was coming, and that braying laugh couldn't belong to anyone other than Arlene Schmidt—the biggest gossip in town. To make matters worse, she was malicious. That took the decision out of my hands.

"Shut up," I hissed, slamming the stall door closed and effectively hiding us from the newcomers. "Be very, very quiet.

Bunny responded with a moan.

Arlene and her friends spent an interminable amount of time conducting their ablutions. No wonder. Arlene bore an uncanny resemblance to a quarter horse. She needed all the mirror time she could get.

Where had *that* come from? I hadn't been catty in almost twenty years. Was I having a relapse?

Finally, finally, finally, Arlene and company left in a cloud of hairspray and nose-clogging perfume.

"Let's get out of here." I helped Bunny to her feet and steered her past the mirror.

"I look horrible," she moaned. "See this?" She stretched the skin around her eyes. "I need to have some work done."

"Oh, for goodness sake! That is so *dumb*. You're a beautiful woman. You don't need plastic surgery." I handed her a wet paper towel. My purse was the size of a postage stamp, so all I could provide was a little powder and lipstick.

"You're a good friend, you know that? I haven't had a friend since high school."

That made me feel about as tall as a Lilliputian.

"Yeah, well, uh…" Although I was normally articulate, I found myself at a loss for words.

"The only people I know are snobs, horrible snobs." Bunny emphasized her assertion with a hiccup. "And the biggest one of all is my husband. He didn't want me to come to the reunion, did you know that?"

I shook my head.

"Nope!" She smacked the faucet so hard, water squirted everywhere. "He thinks we're hicks. My daddy could buy and sell him."

Ooh-kay—too much information.

"I didn't tell him I was going to the reunion. I left a note on his golf clubs. He loves that damned putter more than he loves me."

Definitely too much information.

Chapter 22

Miracle of miracles, I managed to make Bunny presentable. "Come on, let's join the others."

"I don't, uh…um."

I knew exactly what the problem was: Bunny didn't have on her perfect hair and makeup. I suspected she'd been relying on that armor for a very long time.

"She's scary." The "she" Bunny was referring to was our friend Misty. And to be honest, she wasn't far off in her assessment.

"She's been our friend forever. Come on, let's go," I said with more confidence than I felt. "Chin up, chest out, smile on." In high school, that had been our secret code for putting on our Brazen Betty disguise—the girl who could bluff her way through anything.

Bunny smiled. She was a tad green around the gills, but she was smiling. What more could I ask from a not-so-happy drunk?

Even from a distance, I could see that Charlie and Bill were not faring so well. In fact, they looked like they were facing a firing squad. Who could blame them? Misty was in rare form, pontificating about one of her favorite causes. What was it about a high-school reunion that brought on the craziness?

It took a few false starts before I finally convinced Bunny to go back to the table with me. She'd noticed Misty's performance, too. We were almost at our destination when Bunny skidded to a stop.

"He's here," she said. It was a classic deer-in-the-headlights moment.

"My husband's here. That's my husband!" The man she indicated was tall, dark and incredibly handsome. He also resembled a Mafia don with slicked-back hair and an expensive Italian suit.

Oh. Lord!

"Angelique," he boomed the minute he spied Bunny. Although he might look like he'd just come from Sicily, his accent was pure Back Bay Boston. I would've bet my 401(k) he went to Harvard.

The arm he put around his wife was more proprietary than affectionate, leading me to wonder if it was safe for her to be alone with him. Not that I could stop either of them if they decided to leave.

"Bunny, are you okay?" I asked.

"She's fine. I'm taking my wife back to the motel." The way he said motel was reminiscent of the time I ate a raw oyster—it left a slimy aftertaste. "She's obviously not feeling too well."

That was true; however, it didn't answer my question.

Charlie saw what was happening and quickly summoned Bill and Misty to join me in creating a united front.

"Everything all right here?" Bill asked.

It was a toss-up as to whether he'd pull out a badge or a gun. I'm sure he was armed. Ditto for Misty. There were plenty of violent felons who'd crossed her off their Christmas card lists.

"Everything's wonderful," Bunny said, plastering on a phony smile.

In the blink of an eye, she'd reverted to Long Island Lucy—society matron.

"Visiting with you has been delightful."

What?

"We'll have to do it again soon. We have a lovely large place with a guesthouse. Please feel free to come by when you're in New York."

She air-kissed me before she marched regally out of the hall on her husband's arm. The queen was back, gone was the vulnerable girl I'd briefly glimpsed.

That was too bad.

"Do you think she's okay?" Charlie asked as we made our way back to the table.

"I guess. What I really think is that her life is miserable. But you can't help someone who doesn't want to be helped."

"Isn't that the truth," he murmured. "Are

you ready to end this part of the evening? I've had about all the reunion I can take."

"Me, too."

"Want to go into San Antonio for dessert and drinks?"

"Good idea," I said, and then had second thoughts. "I'm afraid Mary Alice will have a fit if we all leave."

Misty and Bill had made an abrupt departure following the Bunny debacle. Chickens! They were probably off somewhere comparing guns—or not.

"Stay here. I'll tell Petey what we're doing. He'll be our buffer." Our friend was standing at the edge of the dance floor. Can you say bored silly?

I don't know what Charlie told him; whatever it was, Petey was wearing a huge smile when he waved us toward the door.

"Did I tell you how pretty you are?" Charlie had me pinned up against the car door, nuzzling the tender skin beneath my ear.

"Mmm." Nuzzling was such an underrated skill. And Charlie did it so well. "That is so, um…" As hard as I tried to resist it, a sigh escaped. Could I be any more obvious if I tried? And did I really care?

Nah!

Charlie assisted me into the car, a feat that was easier said than done considering my tight skirt and high heels.

"I have another suggestion, if you're game." He leaned over the console and kissed me before he started the car.

"What?"

"Let's run by the Super Saver and pick up dessert and a bottle of wine. We can take the boat to the lagoon and have some privacy."

That was the best proposition I'd heard in ages.

"Okay." I was agreeing to a lot more than a boat ride in the moonlight, and that was okay; in fact, it was better than okay. It was terrific.

We had bought a Black Forest cake and a bottle of Texas Pinot Noir. What could be more romantic? Chocolate, wine and moonlight?

"Do you think Bunny is safe with her

husband?" Charlie asked as he refilled my plastic glass.

Talk about a mood buster. Even chocolate couldn't take the sting from that question. "If you're referring to her physical well-being, I think she's fine. If you're talking about her happiness, I have my doubts."

Much as I hated it, this required a serious discussion—and just when we were on the way to a new level of understanding.

Shoot!

Charlie flattened the cake icing with his fork. "I feel sorry for her."

"I do, too. She made some terrible decisions."

"That she did." He studied the wine in his glass. "At least I know what happened to the baby." He sighed. "I never forgot. It was always in the back of my mind—did I have a kid somewhere? Was he or she healthy? Happy?"

"Worrying about that must've been a terrible way to live."

"It's okay. It's over," he said, offering me a bite of chocolate icing. There was something incredibly intimate about sharing a fork, especially with Charlie.

"Here's to new beginnings."

"I'll drink to that."

There were a couple of givens in life. The sun would come up the next day. And Charlie and I were about to kiss—and kiss and kiss. What we'd do after the kiss was the question. And the answer was up to me.

Charlie stroked my lower lip with his thumb. "Can you believe it's taken us twenty years to come full circle?"

I was so mesmerized by the look in his eye that I couldn't say a thing.

"Jazz, I loved you then and I love you now." He put his forehead against mine and made soothing little circles on my back, his fingers cool and certain. "What happened to your ring?"

This week with Charlie had been delicious, delightful and disturbing. We'd done nothing more than kiss, but I knew deep down inside that we were about to raise the stakes. "I took it off. I'm giving it back to Dom. I can't marry a man I don't love." As I verbalized my intention, I realized I'd already begun to follow my heart. I no longer considered myself engaged; only the formality of breaking my—arrangement with Dom remained.

With that knowledge came the freedom to put my arms around Charlie's neck. "Make love to me." Initially I whispered my request, but as I grew bolder, so did my demand. "Now, here in the moonlight."

It was one of the few times in our long friendship that I'd astonished him. I would've giggled if we hadn't been discussing something that was going to change our lives.

"Are you sure?" he asked, although his fingers were sliding up my thigh. "Really sure?"

If he planned to yammer on, I'd have to take matters into my own hands. Which I was about to do when he suddenly kissed me senseless. Well, not exactly senseless, because all my senses were on high alert, especially when it came to his talented, talented hand that was creeping higher and higher on my leg toward a very interesting and erotic destination.

Somewhere in the background I could hear frogs singing and the wind sighing through the trees. It was the perfect accompaniment to the best loving I'd had in…well, forever.

As Charlie slowly pulled down my zipper, he used his tongue to work a magic that was euphoric. Somehow, some way, he'd elevated kissing to a work of art. The man was a Renoir.

I was making all kinds of little noises, but I didn't care. Rational thought had long since taken a hike. When Charlie slid the silk straps down my arms and the dress pooled around my waist, the soft night breeze caressed my flesh.

"You are so beautiful," Charlie murmured as he lowered his head to my breasts.

At that moment I felt beautiful and completely feminine.

Nothing in my life had ever felt so right.

Chapter 23

I was in bed luxuriating in dreams of Charlie when the phone rang. The sounds of summer were everywhere—the man next door was mowing his lawn, kids were playing with inner tubes on the river and Mama was singing off tune while she did her gardening.

When my cell jingled again, I fluffed the pillow and popped open my phone.

"Hi, Sunshine."

It was Charlie, of course. There wasn't anyone else in the world who called me Sunshine.

"Have lunch with me?"

"Where?" It was inevitable that I'd say yes, but it never hurt to make him work for it.

"We should go to La Casa."

Wow, La Casa was the most romantic place in the county. "Don't you want to go to the Catfish Shack?"

Charlie chuckled in response.

"Should I get dressed up?"

"That revealing little red sundress would be nice."

Whew—my inner bad girl was rarin' to go!

Although it'd been ages since I'd been to La Casa, it was everything I remembered and more. The flowers were fragrant, the ambiance was wonderful, the food was delicious, the wine was cold, the company was delightful and I was in heaven.

"I love this place," I said as we shared a piece of fresh strawberry pie. "It's so peaceful I could stay here all day."

And it was serene. Until he took my hand

and lobbed a conversational mortar in my direction.

"I love you. You know that, don't you?"

"Uh-huh."

"I want us to get married. Now. Right away."

What was it about men and their unerring bad sense of timing? Marrying Charlie was something I wanted almost as much as I desired my next breath, but I'd just broken up with my fiancé. Or rather, I was in the process of doing so.

"I, uh… I don't think… I need—"

He interrupted me before I could finish my sentence. "What's the problem?" he drawled. "I suppose since I screwed up way back when, you've decided to pay me back by being the dumper this time around."

"What are you talking about? That's not what I was going to say! Don't put words in my mouth." Charlie was feeling insecure about our new relationship and who could blame him? Heck, I was anxious, too.

"Charlie."

He put his hand up. "Let's not discuss this if you're planning to tell me you've changed your mind about us and you're going back to California."

"Charlie!" My voice skittered up an octave and I couldn't do a darned thing about it. He was on the verge of making me *very* mad.

Charlie was accusing me, *me,* of sabotaging our relationship, when I'd changed my entire life to include him. Well, he was about to get it with both barrels. After that, we could make up. Then my cell phone chirped. I definitely had to change that ring tone!

I gave him a squinty-eyed look of disapproval as I checked the caller ID. It was Dom. I had a weird feeling I should answer it.

"I have to take this. We'll finish our discussion when I get back," I warned him, snapping open my phone and walking toward the edge of the patio.

"Hello, Dom."

"Jasmine, you need to come home. Dad is extremely ill and he wants to talk to you."

"Is he going to…" I couldn't complete the question. I already knew the answer. Santo wouldn't ask me to come back unless there wasn't much time left.

"He's not going to make it."

"Do you know what he wants to tell me?"

There was a pause before he answered. "His dying wish is that we get married. Tomorrow if possible. He says that if he can be at the wedding, he'll die a happy man."

I wanted to scream and howl at the moon. Could I really tell my friend, my mentor, my surrogate father *no?* How could life be so unfair? Just when I had a chance to grab the brass ring, this had to happen.

What was my next step? Give up Charlie? Not an option. Disappoint Santo, a man who was more than a friend? Couldn't do that, either.

"I'll book a ticket and let you know when I'll be there." The shock was too new for me to even cry. I knew Santo had been sick, but I had a hard time figuring out how a stomach ailment had become a terminal disease. After I hung up, I wandered down to the creek to get control of my emotions. I didn't want this tragedy to spill over into the conversation I had to have with Charlie. When

I could talk without breaking into tears, I went back to our table.

"Charlie, I have to go to California. Today. That call was from Dom. He said his dad's dying. I don't have any choice but to go home."

Charlie obviously wasn't tuned in to what I was saying. "All right, if that's the way it is, let's get you home so you can pack." He stood abruptly and threw some money on the table. "Are you coming?" he asked, already marching out of the restaurant.

The silence in the car was suffocating. I tried more than once to start a conversation, but each time I opened my mouth he cut me off with a glare.

Finally I'd had enough. "Stop the car."

That got Charlie's attention. He whipped over to the side of the road and slammed the transmission into Park.

"What?"

"I told you Santo's dying and he wants me to marry Dom right away."

Charlie turned in the seat and gave me a hard look. "So what do you plan to do about us?"

I paused, trying to think of a solution, but apparently it took me too long to formulate a response.

"That's what I suspected," Charlie said. His voice was grim. "Damn it. That's what I thought." He shifted into Drive and hit the gas. "I hoped we had a chance." He laughed. It was a cynical sound devoid of humor. "I guess we're just another Romeo and Juliet."

If I couldn't make Charlie listen, I didn't have a chance of persuading him to understand. I had to have some time. I wanted Charlie to trust me. Was that being unreasonable?

"I can't believe you'd marry a man you don't love. Yes, I understand how you feel about Santo, but if he cares about *you,* he won't expect you to go through with this." He pulled into my parents' driveway and stopped the car. "If you change your mind, call me. But remember, I've waited a lifetime for you and I'm not willing to wait much longer."

There was only one answer I could come up with. "I love you. I'm not planning to marry Dom." I was pleading but I couldn't help myself. "We can work this out. We can."

He shot me another look as I got out of the car. He seemed just as devastated as I was.

"Call me when you decide that being with me is what really matters to you."

Charlie drove off before I could respond. How could he be so hardheaded and unreasonable? I'd told him all about Dom and Santo. He knew how much Santo meant to me; he'd even admitted that. How could he be so unfeeling? Why wasn't he comforting me instead of driving away? If you asked my brain, I had the answer. He wasn't quite sure of me yet. But my heart was screaming that he should trust me.

I knew he'd heard only about half of what I'd said. Did he really think I'd marry a man I didn't love?

Was my relationship with Charlie that fragile? If he truly loved me, he would've moved heaven and earth to make this work.

"Damn it!" I screeched as I stomped in to pack a bag.

It wasn't until I was on the plane to California that I decided we weren't fated to be together, after all.

Summer 2007

Chapter 24

"Mother!" Interesting how a simple word accompanied by a whine was enough to give a mom a migraine. How could a kid who was learning calculus at thirteen sound like such a brat?

"Yes, Rayna."

"I want to go back to California. My dad will let me live with him." She didn't stomp her foot, even though she was obviously tempted.

"And I want a belly-button ring." Uh-huh. Now we'd reached the crux of the matter.

My plan for the afternoon was to veg out

on Mama's dock. I had a glass of iced tea, a good book and a sun hat. What more could a woman want? Oh, right. Privacy.

Reluctantly, I put the novel in my lap. "We've discussed this over and over. By the end of the summer, I'll make up my mind about our future plans. And don't worry—you'll get a fair shot at expressing your opinion."

"The kids here are all dorks," Rayna wailed.

Unfortunately, she'd made that same pronouncement every day since we'd landed at the San Antonio airport. And that had been three very long weeks ago.

In an effort to preserve my sanity, I'd decided to ignore her. It wasn't a chapter in the supermoms' handbook, but if it worked, it worked.

Not getting the kind of reaction she wanted, Rayna marched back to the house and slammed the door. You had to give the kid credit; she was an expert at dramatic exits. High dudgeon seemed to be de rigueur for a kid at the beginning of the tempestuous teens. I hoped I'd survive.

And speaking of dramatic exits—why hadn't *I* left California in a spectacular fit of pique instead of stealing away in the night? When I found Dom with his secretary (how's that for a cliché?) doing the dirty on top of his Lucite desk, I'd been sorely tempted to pull a Lorena Bobbitt. Really, I had.

Instead, I'd lapsed into my good-girl demeanor and hired the best shark in town. It turned out—lucky for me—that my lawyer and CPA were better than his lawyer and CPA, and financially I was doing fine. Mentally, I wasn't quite so sure.

It'd been two years since that fateful day, and here I was—a perimenopausal single mom with a kid whose main goal in life was to have purple highlights and a belly-button ring. My divorce had been tempestuous, devastating, exhausting.

For many women, a traumatic life change heralded an incredible weight loss, or conversely, you ended up with a waddle reminiscent of Dumbo. During the height of the fiasco, everything I put in my mouth tasted like cardboard. So, needless to say, I fell into the former category.

Now I was back home in Texas. The way I figured, if it didn't work out, I could at least spend the summer eating comfort food, licking my wounds and deciding what I wanted to do when I grew up. So far, my only epiphany was that trooping back to the nest as a fifty-year-old was harder and more disconcerting than I'd expected.

When Daddy died of a sudden heart attack in the middle of my divorce, I felt as if I'd been set adrift. Losing him was tough, and it took me a long time to come to terms with his death. Now Mama was ready to move to a condo in town and I was seriously considering buying our family river house and following my dream of an art career.

Although Rayna and I had discussed a Texas move—ad nauseam—she preferred to do the teenage thing and pretend it wasn't going to happen. She had a vote, but I was the ultimate decision maker. And before I did anything rash—like call a moving van—I wanted to see how we'd both fare in small-town Texas.

The jury was still out on that one.

"Hey, Jazzy. Petey agreed to take the girls on a shopping expedition tomorrow." Mary Alice paused, then muttered, "I'm on the phone."

Mothers all over the world were familiar with that refrain. What was it about kids that the minute you picked up a phone, they had a 911 emergency?

"Just a sec, I need to find out where Lily's going." There was some muffled conversation and then she returned. "Okay, I'm back. Anyway, I thought Rayna might like to come along. Dahlia would love her company."

Mary Alice and Petey's four girls ranged from twelve to twenty-two. It was a darned good thing they hadn't tried for a fifth, because they probably would've named her Nasturtium. Wouldn't *that* be worth a few years on the therapist's couch?

"Sounds good to me." In fact, it sounded fantastic. "She's next door. I'll ask her when she gets home." This was a no-brainer. Rayna would jump at the chance to go back to the civilized world of malls and food courts. The bonus for me was that she'd be forty miles away without a cell phone.

"I don't know about you, but the combination of summer vacation and children makes me crazy," Mary Alice said.

Considering that she was a charter member of the soccer-mom club, that was an astonishing admission.

"I think we should go out for lunch and have lots and lots of wine," she continued. "We haven't had a girl talk since you got home."

Adult conversation, wine, good food— that was my idea of heaven. In the three weeks I'd been in Texas, I hadn't seen anyone other than Rayna and Mama, and to be completely honest they'd both fallen off my favorite folks list.

"I'm ready." Was I ever!

"How about Alberto's tomorrow at noon?" she suggested.

"I'll be there."

* * *

"Jazzy, sweetie, I'm going to dinner with my bridge group," Mama announced as she walked through the living room later that afternoon.

"And I have a sleepover," Rayna piped up. "You remember that, don't you?"

"Yes, I know." Rayna and Cissy Aldrich, the girl next door, were inching their way toward friendship, and that was the best news I'd had in a long time. Making new friends was the only thing that would change her attitude toward Meadow Lake.

Mama and Rayna left for their respective activities and I was stuck with a bowl of popcorn and a DVD. Was it possible to be a wallflower at fifty?

"Darn," I muttered, searching the kitchen cabinets for the bottle of wine I'd seen a couple of days ago. Did I drink it?

"Jeez," I groused. Grousing had become my preferred form of communication.

As I grabbed the car keys from the foyer table, I accidentally caught a brief glance in the mirror.

Good gosh! I looked like a refugee from

a swap meet. What in the world had happened to the woman who could walk confidently into a roomful of professional men, guys wearing thousand-dollar suits?

She was obviously on vacation.

Well, crap! I pulled my hair up into a Pebbles ponytail, smeared on some lip gloss and called it good. I was only going to the grocery store for a bottle of wine—never mind that in Meadow Lake the Super Saver was the hub of civilization.

Sure enough, the parking lot was crammed with cars. What? They were having a run on dairy products? Since it was Friday night, more than likely it was a run on beer—beer they'd take to a party, a party I wasn't invited to. Yikes! Self-induced pity was *so* disgusting.

In my previous life I didn't have time for a wasted trip to the store, and habits die hard, so I grabbed a cart and went through a mental inventory of things we needed.

I headed straight to the Snickers aisle and grabbed a bag. Pigging out on chocolate sounded like a wee bit of paradise— Snickers, chocolate-brownie ice cream with caramel, or even double-fudge Keeblers. If I didn't get off my current binge, my butt was going to end up broader than a barn door. Jeez! The longer I hung out in the Lone Star state, the more I thought in Texan-isms.

So instead of whacking myself upside the head—there it was again—I did the adult thing and wheeled my cart through the produce section. The melons were plump. The peaches were juicy. The oranges, well, they were orange, and there wasn't a single solitary item in the whole section that produced endorphins. Those wonderful, wonderful endorphins.

I was fantasizing about yummy chocolate when my good-mother conscience made a belated appearance. I tossed some fruit in my cart and headed over to the meat department, where I found a huge display of *menudo*. Only in south Texas would packages of cow's stomach be snuggled up next to a selection of pot roasts. That was one delicacy I could skip.

So far, I hadn't seen a soul I recognized. But the wine and beer aisle was another story. Friday night, small Texas town, six-packs of Shiner Bock—yep, half the town was perusing the refrigerated beer counter.

Oh, well, in for a penny, and all that. I maneuvered the cart toward my destination. By that time I wasn't picky; I'd take practically anything in a bottle with a cork. I drew the line at screw tops.

I'd just grabbed a bottle of Fredericksburg white when I heard that *voice*.

"Jazzy, what are you doing here?"

My world was about to be spun on its axis again. Slowly, very slowly, I turned and there he was, Charlie Morrison in all his blond, still broad-shouldered, handsome glory. And speaking of wine, that man had aged like a fine merlot.

Through all the ups and downs of life with Dom, I'd never been able to get Charlie out of my mind. I'd start thinking about him, wondering where he was, *how* he was. Unfortunately, I'd been too chicken to ask anyone about him. The truth was, I didn't want to know what I'd missed. Now suddenly, he was standing right in front of me. He was still gorgeous, and I was…I was.

"Hi, Charlie," I squeaked. "I'm buying

some wine." Like an idiot I held up the bottle, but before I could say anything else, he enveloped me in a huge hug. It was an action that drew stares from some of the people who were studying the selection of Napa Valley products. Since when had hugging in public become taboo?

"It's good to see you." He held me at arm's length and took a look. "Are you here on vacation?"

The rumor mill obviously hadn't burped out my sordid story to the *entire* populace.

"Well, sort of and sort of not. I'm testing the waters." I didn't explain what I meant by that comment.

He laughed and I was delighted to discover that he still had that wonderful belly laugh—the one I remembered so well and realized I'd missed so desperately. The memory of that sound had sustained me through the darkest years of my divorce.

"Here." He took the bottle out of my hand, put it in the cart and took command. "Let's check out and head over to the Chocolate Cow, my treat. We have a lot to get caught up on."

Charlie and my grocery cart were halfway to the checkout stand before I'd closed my mouth, much less summoned a cogent thought.

Good grief! This was not a rational girl's daydream. Because in a fantasy, I would've looked like a million dollars—not like a dollar-store babe.

Chapter 25

I'm still not sure why Charlie was at the Super Saver that fateful day. But I wasn't about to question a gift from the gods.

Was it our destiny to meet summer after summer—even if those summers were decades apart? Was this our chance to finally get it right? I'd noticed he wasn't wearing a wedding ring. Had he noticed that I wasn't, either?

I suppose I agreed to go with him, although I don't think I ever actually formed the words. I suspect I nodded a couple of times; however, I'm not positive about that, either. It's a good thing he was willing to keep the conversation rolling.

Charlie loaded my groceries in the minuscule trunk of Mama's Mini Cooper and tossed me the keys.

"Cute car. It's kinda small, though."

"Yeah, well. It's Mama's. If I decide to stay, I'll probably buy an SUV." Was I babbling and did he really need to know that?

"*Are* you staying?"

The parking lot was so hot it felt as if the asphalt was searing the soles of my feet. Not to mention that the little makeup I had on was melting and my ponytail was drooping like a wet mop.

"It's a long story. Let's go to the restaurant—at least it's air-conditioned—and I'll tell you everything."

He gave another one of those laughs. I could get addicted to that sound.

"Your car or mine?"

Was that a double entendre? Not with my luck, it wasn't.

"Mine," I said.

"Okay, if you promise you'll winch me out of this thing," he said with a chuckle, folding his long legs into an unnatural position. "I feel like I'm in a clown car."

I zipped into the flow of traffic. The car might be small, but it could move.

"I see your driving hasn't changed."

I spared him a glance as I whizzed by a cement truck. Was that a compliment or an insult? And did I want to get into an argument with him before we even got past the "what have you been doing for the last fourteen years" part of the conversation? No, I really wanted to know what he'd done with his life.

"It comes from living in California. What's life without a couple of high-speed car chases a day?"

"You got me there," he said, surreptitiously checking his seat belt.

"I have a better idea than the Chocolate Cow," I said, although I wasn't sure my suggestion was wise.

"I'm yours."

Wouldn't that be nice? Or was I about to embroil myself in another emotional mess?

Relationships, to put it mildly, were not my forte.

My first thought was to head straight to the old dam. But I had to say "whoa, girl" to that. So instead, I drove down River Road and found a deserted picnic table. It offered privacy, without being *too* private.

It wasn't until I'd parked under a sprawling live oak that Charlie made any comment. "Do you have a corkscrew to open that bottle of wine?" He carefully extracted himself from the car.

"Yep, and I also have chips and salsa." I produced the snacks with a flourish. I might've skimped on the healthy food, but I hadn't bypassed the junk.

I really had to watch out for that barn door.

Charlie put his arm around my shoulders and together we strolled to the table.

Chips and salsa were perfect for an impromptu picnic. Simply rip open the bag and eat. The wine was more of a problem. Opening it was easy; cups were another matter. Slurping it out of the bottle was tacky.

"I'll check the car to see if there's anything we can use." Bingo, there was a mug in the cup holder. It wasn't quite clean and it definitely wasn't up to Martha Stewart's standards (or mine), but sometimes a girl had to improvise.

"Look what I found."

"I have the wine open." Charlie sloshed some golden liquid into the cup in a vain attempt to get rid of the coffee residue. "I guess we'll have to share, huh?"

"Yep, there won't be any toasts. Not unless we clink our heads together."

"I pass, at least on the head-butting," Charlie said as he poured the wine and let me take the first sip.

Not bad, not bad at all. In fact, it was a mighty fine combination—a chilled chardonnay, chips and salsa, a relatively cool breeze and a very hot man. Things could definitely be worse.

Charlie leaned back against the table and stretched out his long legs. "So, in twenty-five words or less, what have you been doing for the last fourteen years?"

Charlie always got straight to the point.

It felt like a dam burst, releasing a flood of feelings. All it took was a simple question and I was more than ready to spill my guts.

We talked—actually I did most of the talking—for more than an hour. In the process, we consumed most of the wine. By the time I finally ran down, he'd heard our family saga—the good, the bad and the indifferent.

"Well," I said as I slugged back more vino. "I suppose my monologue fell in the category of too much information."

"No way." He chuckled. "But you did hog the wine."

"I did, didn't I?" I'd been so engrossed in talking I hadn't noticed what else I was doing. Whoa, I was tipsy.

"Yeah, you did. I remember you were a cute drunk," Charlie said, skillfully repairing my ponytail.

I was impressed. "I suppose you know how to do that because you're a pediatrician." What was I thinking? The man probably had a houseful of daughters. And I wanted to find out....

I shoved the almost empty bottle and the cup at him. "There. It's your turn. Confession time." That was supposed to be a demand. The accompanying giggle, however, diminished my credibility.

"I moved back about five years ago and went into practice with a friend from medical school. I'm on staff at the county hospital."

"Really?"

His grin caught me off guard. My tummy was doing flip-flops again.

"No kidding. I bought the blue Victorian on the corner of University Boulevard and State Street. You remember the one, don't you?"

"That's a great house. So why did you move back to Meadow Lake? And why didn't anyone let me know?" Darn it! Mama or Mary Alice should have warned me Charlie was in town. Why did they keep *that* quiet?

"The first question I can answer. As for the second, I don't have any idea. It's certainly not a secret. I see Mary Alice and Petey all the time. But you haven't been home since the funeral, have you?"

"No. I was so busy feeling sorry for myself that I didn't do much traveling, except for business. Plus, Rayna spends a lot of time with her dad in the summer, so it was hard to get away. Now I realize I was acting like a selfish twit. I should've come home to help Mama."

Charlie responded with an eloquent shrug.

"Why didn't you attend Daddy's funeral?" His presence would've been very comforting, but how would he have known that? I was, after all, the one who'd left him.

"I wasn't sure you'd want me there. I'm really sorry about your dad. He was a nice guy."

"He was, wasn't he? I miss him." This conversation was heading toward some very uncomfortable ground, so I decided to change the subject. "Tell me about your family."

"I have a son named Alex. He's ten and he keeps me on my toes."

It was obvious that Charlie adored this boy.

"Jaz, do you realize we'll be worrying about our kids till the day we're carried off feet first?"

He was right. Parenthood wasn't simply a matter of making it through the first eighteen years. Although with Rayna, my chances of even surviving her adolescence seemed doubtful.

"I hadn't thought of it that way. Thanks for the positive reinforcement."

"And knowing you, you're dying to ask me about a wife, aren't you?"

I was. I assumed divorce, but I wanted the details. "Yep."

From the way his mood changed, I knew this story would not have a happy ending. "About a year and a half after that fiasco we called a high-school reunion, I married another doctor. Susan was fantastic." A nostalgic look flitted across his face. "She was a surgeon on staff at my hospital in Denver, so professionally we had a lot in common. We loved each other, Alex was a delight, and we had great careers. What more could we want?"

He peered into the empty coffee cup. "Then almost six years ago, she was killed in a car wreck. Sometimes, late at night, I used to think it should've been me. That way, Alex would still have a mother."

"Oh, Charlie." My first impulse was to

burst into tears—and then to throw my arms around him. Somehow, I wasn't sure either reaction was appropriate. "I'm so sorry," I whispered.

"So am I," he said. It looked as if he was trying to shake off a disturbing memory. "Alex and I had a hard time. For a while things were really rocky, but we persevered. About a year after the accident, we moved back so my parents could be a bigger part of our lives. I wanted Alex to get to know his extended family. Susan's folks live in Arizona. They're elderly and weren't really capable of providing me with a support system." He flashed me a grin. "Most of the time Alex is a great kid but he has his moments."

I was familiar with that feeling. Most—revise that to *some*—of the time Rayna was a great kid, too. I had high hopes that when the pesky teenage hobgoblins let go of her mind, she'd return to being the wonderful person I knew she was. It was a matter of time and patience—Rayna's time and my patience.

"So, that's our life," he said. "There's really not much to tell. Although I work a lot, I still manage to spend plenty of time with Alex. Other than Mary Alice and Petey, I don't have much of a social life." He gave me a look I couldn't quite interpret. "I bought the land down by the dam. Eventually I plan to build a house there."

"Wow! That's, uh, that's interesting." Interesting, and perhaps more than a little significant?

"I have special…feelings about that place. When it went up for sale, I put in an offer."

The best memories of my life were entwined with Charlie and our secret place. In the darkest part of the night—and when I was totally honest with myself—I knew I'd always been in love with him. He was the one person in the world who could bring out the best in me. The one person who made me feel complete—and completely loved.

But right now I had a few other priorities—small items like creating a new life, buying a house, dealing with pubescent hormones and last, but certainly not least, facing menopause.

Ye gods!

Chapter 26

"Why didn't you tell me Charlie was back in town?" I thought Mama had made her peace with him years ago, but maybe I was wrong.

She was bustling around the kitchen making Rayna her favorite strawberry waffles. Lord, that woman was spoiling my daughter. Breakfast at our California house was usually a choice between Frosted Flakes and Cheerios, not waffles and French toast.

It took her a few seconds to answer.

"I didn't think it would matter. As a matter of fact—" she sat down across the table from me "—when you left town after the re-union, we felt you'd divorced yourself completely from any life you had here."

Coming from my mother, that was a low blow. It was true, but she wasn't playing fair. The months following my return to California—way back when—had been a blur of meshing the past with the future.

Two weeks after I got back, Dom and I were married at the hospital chapel. He'd actually wanted to do it the very next day, but I'd insisted my parents be there. And they were. But Daddy and Mama looked like they were attending a funeral rather than a wedding ceremony. Santo, on the other hand, was beaming.

Within the next month my friend and mentor was dead, and I was left facing the future with a man I didn't love. Dom and I were great business partners. Our marriage left a lot to be desired.

"You still should've told me." I savagely buttered a slice of toast.

"I didn't, so get over it," Mama responded.

Get over it? That didn't sound like *my* mother. Get over it?

Had she been the victim of an alien abduction? She *was* acting weird. First, there was the condo idea and then she'd bought the Mini Cooper. The biggest surprise of all was her spiky platinum hairdo and new wardrobe.

"Mary Alice and I discussed it, and we decided you didn't need to know, especially with everything you had on your plate," she said over her shoulder as she went into the other room to call Rayna to breakfast.

She was right about my overloaded plate. There were times a turkey platter wouldn't have been sufficient. But Mary Alice and I were definitely overdue for a chat.

Mary Alice jumped at the chance for lunch. The poor woman didn't know I had an ulterior motive. She was thinking about nachos and a margarita.

"I'm leaving now." Rayna and Mama were down on the dock sunning. It was strange; they were acting more like girlfriends than grandmother and granddaughter.

I thought about that as I drove to Mary Alice's store, but came to no conclusions. I was both mother and daughter—and the one in the middle. The one they *both* turned on.

Watching the heat shimmer in Mary Alice's parking lot, I wondered whether I'd taken complete leave of my senses. I pulled into the only available spot and fumbled around in the backseat for that little screen people put in the front window to keep their steering wheels from melting. The longer I drove the Mini, the more I coveted a big, roomy, gas-guzzling SUV.

The cool air of the boutique was almost enough to revive me. My shirt was damp, my ponytail at half-mast, and my makeup was suspect, but at least I could breathe.

I wandered through the racks of clothes as Mary Alice waited on a customer. You had to hand it to M.A.; she was the mistress of hometown chitchat. In the thirty minutes it took Betsy Arnold to decide on a blouse, I learned everything there was to know about her ungrateful kids, and even worse, her plantar warts.

"Hey, sweetie." Mary Alice gave me a hug and then frowned. "What's up?"

Before I could answer, she insulted me.

"How about I get you an appointment with my hairdresser?"

If we hadn't been friends forever, I would've smacked her, even if she was right. I had been remiss in my grooming, and that was something I planned to rectify.

"The ponytail has to go?"

"Definitely," she agreed a bit too vehemently. "And—" she fingered the lapel of my heavy linen blouse "—you need something more appropriate for the climate."

She was right about that, too. In a matter of months, my fashion sense had degenerated.

"Show me what you have."

Mary Alice was an impressive saleswoman. By the time she was finished, I was the proud owner of a completely new wardrobe.

"That was exhausting." I suspected when she added up my total I'd become apoplectic. The stuff in Mary Alice's shop was not cheap—cute but pricey.

"After I get these things wrapped, let's go for nachos."

"Sure. We need to talk."

"Ouch. That sounds ominous."

"It's not too bad." To be completely honest, I understood why she'd squirreled away the information about Charlie. First of all, it wasn't any of my business. And for the past half-dozen years, I'd been a basket case. Trying to keep a floundering marriage together wasn't easy. Neither was dealing with an ugly divorce—and an angry daughter.

Not only that, I'd abandoned Charlie, so why would anyone think that what he did, or didn't do, would be of interest to me?

But in all those years Charlie had never been far from my thoughts. What was he doing? Who was he doing it with? Sometimes I felt like a woman possessed.

I'd made some hard choices, and many times during the intervening years, I'd regretted them. But although confusion was my frequent companion, I knew they were *my* choices and I had to live with them. There was one other thing I knew. I wasn't about to make another life-changing mistake.

No, siree. Not this girl. Not this time.

"Why didn't you tell me Charlie came back to Meadow Lake?" My mouth seemed to have a mind of its own, and it wanted an immediate answer.

Mary Alice looked me straight in the eye and blasted me to smithereens.

"I didn't tell you because you didn't deserve to know. After you hauled ass out of here, we had to help Charlie pick up the pieces. What was wrong with you, anyway?"

"Why don't we discuss this over a drink?" I suggested sheepishly.

"Perhaps we should." Mary Alice slammed the drawer of the cash register. "Margie, watch the store. I'll be back in a couple of hours," she told her employee. "That should do it. We'll either kill each other or we'll be stinkin' drunk."

Two hours later, we'd thrashed out three decades of slights, misunderstandings and grievances. Quiet, calm Mary Alice went for the jugular in listing all the summers I'd flitted in and out of town, expecting to be greeted as the prodigal daughter, and then disappearing again, with only an occasional phone call or e-mail to keep the friendship alive.

All I could say to that was yep, I was guilty.

But the most damaging allegation she made was that I'd broken Charlie's heart.

Damn! I'd really hurt him, and I didn't know how to fix it. Not that I expected to resurrect our relationship, at least not anytime soon, but I had to ask the question.

"Do you think he still feels anything for me?" That question sounded pathetic, even to my ears.

She thought for moment before she responded. "I'm not sure. But if you encourage him and then slink back to Golden Gate country, I'll personally come out there and kill you. Your demise will be nasty and very painful. That's a promise, and I never go back on a promise—or a threat."

She was doing her best Dirty Harriet impression. The image of Mary Alice as a stone-cold killer sent me into gales of laughter.

Mary Alice, being Mary Alice, joined me. We hugged, we made up and we were friends again. We were also plastered.

I collected my shopping bag of new clothes and called the only cab in town. Mary Alice walked—make that weaved— back to the boutique. There was going to be hell to pay when Petey discovered what we'd done all afternoon.

Thank goodness Mama and Rayna were out shopping. I wasn't being a positive role model for an impressionable thirteen-year-old, and Mama—well, let's just say I'd never hear the end of it.

So I'd just staggered up the stairs and flopped on the bed when my cell phone rang.

"Hey, it's Charlie."

It felt almost as if I'd conjured him up.

"Hi."

"Where are you?" I'd bet my last dollar that *he* wasn't out drinking margaritas.

He responded with a chuckle. "Right this

minute I'm at the hospital, but I'm about to head back to my clinic. I hate to ask so late, but the director of pediatrics just asked me to attend a fancy dinner party tonight in his place. Can I talk you into going with me?"

"I don't know." Would I be sober by evening?

"Please? I don't want to go by myself."

I sighed.

"This little fun event will be at the president of the hospital board's house," he said in a wheedling tone. "We're hitting up the board to have a big fund-raiser for an upgrade to the pediatrics unit."

"Oh, okay. What do I have to wear?"

"Something dressy. What do I know about clothes? I'll be wearing a suit."

"What time?"

"Let's say six."

That didn't leave a lot of time for recuperation and repair. Not to mention I had to figure out what to wear. I had a whole pile of new clothes. Unfortunately, those garments ran more to sassy sundresses and cheeky capris than "let's meet the head of the hospital board" attire.

"Okay." I sighed again. "Six it is."

Would I ever be able to say no to Charlie?

Oh, that's right—I *had* said no to the most important question anyone had ever asked me. I'm smart, I know I am, lots of people realize I am, but sometimes I astonish myself with my stupid decisions.

Chapter 27

"Have you been here before?" Charlie asked as he pulled into the circular driveway of Mr. and Mrs. Dunwoody's home. It was the largest mansion in town.

"Are you kidding? Visiting someone at this house would've been like having tea with God. Good thing I decided against wearing jeans, huh?"

"Yes," he agreed.

Charlie's exquisitely tailored charcoal-gray suit fit him to perfection. Now if only I could keep from salivating. He cut the engine and kissed me. "You look lovely to-night."

"Thanks." I had to chuckle because Charlie's invitation had sent me scurrying back to the boutique—in a cab, of course. Mary Alice was super cranky and my only consolation was that she seemed to be in worse shape than I was. We did, however, find a great outfit—a beige silk jacket and pants with a rust silk tank. I felt quite spiffy and sexy and attractive, better than I had in years.

Charlie came around to help me out of the car, not that I was incapable of opening the door, but Texas guys are consummate gentlemen. He held my hand as we walked up to a massive front door. It was a simple show of affection, but it made me feel young, reminding me of long-ago summers.

The ostentatious setting was the right backdrop for the Lurch look-alike who answered the door in full butler regalia. We were still in south Texas, weren't we?

"I'm Dr. Morrison and this is Mrs. Rinaldi." Charlie managed to introduce us without laughing. I don't think I could've pulled that one off.

Since I'd lived in California for so long, the importance of local aristocracy escaped me. I was used to dealing with people who were far wealthier than these folks. Believe me, international real estate development doesn't come cheap. Unfortunately, the movers and shakers of Meadow Lake weren't aware of the finite nature of their fiefdom.

The dinner was going well, everything considered. Charlie was his usual charming self, and I was doing okay in the face of incredible snobbery. Just mention California and our hostess's face screwed up as if she'd been sucking on a lemon.

The truly ironic thing was that Californians thought Texans were hicks of the highest (or would that be lowest?) order. Jeez! Blue states, red states, East Coast, West Coast, fly-over country—who really cares? What difference does it make?

We'd just started the entrée when disaster struck. I wasn't paying a whole lot of attention when the butler/cook/or whatever he was served the Cornish hens. You had to give him credit; he was polished enough to get a gig at Buckingham Palace.

I'm not a huge fan of little chickens that are not only hard to eat but couldn't satisfy the appetite of a gnome. When I stuck a fork in that sucker he slid—no, he almost sailed—off the plate, hitting me square in chest, and then the little bugger fell in my lap. All conversation ceased as everyone at the table, in unison, stared at the huge greasy spot. I realized rust silk was not the best fabric in the world to hide a stain, and *that* was an understatement.

Even Lurch was caught in a state of suspended animation. That is, until I began to laugh. I tried to control myself, but every time I looked at the grease blob, I broke into howls of hilarity. I laughed so hard my eyes watered and my stomach hurt. A few of the braver guests started giggling. And then Mrs. Dunwoody made a comment that reduced me to tears of laughter.

"Chester, would you please bring Mrs. Rinaldi a bib."

* * *

Charlie and I barely made it out of the driveway before he pulled over and joined me in my semihysterical state.

"God, that was funny," he said between chuckles.

"Did you see the look on Lurch's face?"

"Oh, yeah."

"I hope I didn't mess up anything for you or for the pediatrics folks," I said anxiously.

"Don't worry about it. If the board members don't have a sense of humor, we'll figure out something else." Charlie emphasized his comment by tangling his fingers in my hair and pulling me across the console for a toe-curling kiss.

Wow! *That* I could get used to.

After several minutes of erotic indulging, he leaned back and sighed. "I want to ask you something. And before you immediately say no, think about it."

Warning flags went up all over the place.

"Would you go to the coast with me for the weekend? Wait." He raised one hand like a traffic cop. "I promise to be a gentleman. I won't try to pressure you into anything.

A friend from college and I own a beach house at the Gulf. You can have all the privacy you want."

I wasn't sure I wanted privacy, or space, or anything else that didn't include Charlie.

"Think about it and let me know tomorrow."

I was fifty-one years old. It was time to loosen up and live dangerously.

"I don't have to think about it. I'd love to go."

"That was easier than I thought it'd be." He sealed our deal with another kiss.

Chapter 28

The next week proved to be a combination of calm and nerve-racking excitement. The tranquility was the result of Rayna's falling into a routine of water-skiing and hanging out with Mary Alice's daughters, as well as the girl next door. The anticipation came from my alternating feelings of "I can't wait," and "What have I agreed to do?" Now Saturday was actually here.

I was preparing for the trip and Mary Alice was making herself at home on my bed amid a growing pile of discarded clothes. A trip to the beach meant wearing a bathing suit—in public. At my age.

"Of course I packed a suit," I said in answer to her question. "It's summer and we're going to the beach." I didn't tell her I wasn't about to wade any higher than my kneecaps. No siree, creepy crawly things of every hue and description lived in the ocean—sharks, manta rays, jellyfish and Man o' War, to mention just a few. The Gulf was nothing like the tame little river of my youth.

Truthfully, I was more nervous about Charlie than I was about the sharks. Why was I so on edge?

That was easy to answer. I'd never gone off with a guy for the weekend, not even with Dom before we were married. How could anyone my age be so clueless about dating protocol?

"I think it's a great idea for you and Charlie to take a little R & R at the beach," M.A. was saying. "Don't worry about Rayna. Your mom and I will look after her. All you need to do is relax and enjoy yourself."

Easy for her to say. She wasn't about to get stuck in a romantic, out-of-the-way beach house with Dr. Testosterone. It was one thing to be *thinking* about hanky-panky. Doing it was another thing entirely. The weekend smacked way too much of a honeymoon, and that thought led straight to the subject of marriage.

Where in heaven's name had the M-word come from?

"In general I'm not sure our trip is a good idea. And specifically, I don't feel I'm prepared for...whatever."

"Are you about ready?" Charlie called from the bottom of the stairs. "If we leave right this minute, we can make it before dinner."

"Coming," I shouted, slamming the lid on my suitcase. If I didn't have what I needed, I could always buy it. After all, we were only going to the beach for a couple of days. It was the nights that worried me.

"Come down with me," I begged Mary Alice. "You might have to push me into the car."

My so-called friend made clucking noises all the way into the kitchen, where Mama stood chatting with Charlie. She'd handed him a huge plate of chocolate cake.

"That was delicious," he said, forking up the last crumb. "Is your daughter as great a cook as you are?"

"No," I told him. "I don't even own a cake pan."

Charlie laughed and chucked me under the chin.

"I fixed a basket of food for the trip. It's on the table in the sunroom," Mama said.

The way everyone was acting, you'd think we were heading out in a Conestoga instead of taking a two-hour trip in a TrailBlazer.

We took the meandering back way to the coast, which allowed us plenty of time to talk. It was astonishing that we could spend hours together and never run out of subjects to discuss. And even more astonishing, we were also good at companionable silence.

The narrow two-lane highway wound through a series of small towns dotted with mom-and-pop diners and no-name motels. Bubba's Bait and Beer had a huge sign out front advertising hubcaps, pecans and worms. Rural south Texas hadn't changed much, at least on the surface, in the past four decades.

The land closest to the Gulf was flat, and on a clear day you could see for miles and miles. The only blemish on the landscape was an occasional industrial complex, but what's a humongous chemical plant between friends?

A small ferry took us across the Intracoastal Waterway, depositing us on Mustang Island, the largest barrier island in the world. Miraculously, this part of Texas had largely escaped the onslaught of multistoried tourist hotels so common in beach areas.

This little piece of Gulf Coast paradise reveled in miles of sandy beaches, a gentle sea breeze and dolphins playing in the channel. When we were kids it had been our favorite vacation destination.

Over the years it had become a little more built up, but the basics were the same—the marina, seafood restaurants, boutiques, hotels, and the requisite smattering of T-shirt shops. It was an interesting combination of tourist tacky and Hemingway's Key West.

"Do you come down here often?"

"Only when Alex and I have vacations that mesh, which isn't that frequent. With all their activities, kids are hard to pin down."

I nodded. Other than this summer, I could barely remember the last vacation Rayna and I had taken together. Was the trip to Disney World really the last time we'd had fun?

I was mulling over my maternal shortcomings when Charlie pulled into the driveway of a pale pink house nestled against the sand dunes.

"This is great!"

Constructed of wood and glass, it rested on stilts high enough to compensate for hurricane tidal surges.

Charlie grinned, and I could tell this beach home was his pride and joy. "The second floor has a fantastic ocean view. We can use your mom's care package for a picnic on the deck. I even brought this." He produced a cooler containing chilled bottles of chardonnay.

What a guy!

"Let's go." He hopped out of the car, giving me few options but to follow him, especially since he had the chardonnay.

Leave it to Mama to come up with a picnic fit for a king, or at the very least a country-western star—fried chicken, coleslaw and peach cobbler. You couldn't beat that! After we'd put away the picnic supplies and changed into our swimsuits, Charlie suggested we go for a walk. I suspected he wanted to impress me with the beauty of the beach. And believe me, he succeeded.

We took a leisurely stroll, dipping our toes in the warm Gulf water and stopping periodically to pick up shells and sand dollars. Terns and seagulls swooped all around us, while a brisk breeze tickled our noses with the briny scent of the ocean.

We skirted a group of teenagers involved in a rowdy game of Frisbee and later stopped to watch some toddlers building a sand castle.

"I didn't realize how much I needed this," I commented as I waded into the surf. "My life's been crazy for the past few years. I've been craving some peace and quiet."

Charlie followed me into the water and proceeded to kiss me—and the temperature of the Gulf must've gone up at least ten degrees. That was about as far from calm as a girl could get.

"Do you want to go to a restaurant for dinner or are you up for a bonfire and wiener roast on the beach?" he asked.

"You have driftwood on this beach?"

"Not really, but we could improvise."

"As long as we can do wieners and s'mores, I'm game."

Charlie laughed, putting his arm around my shoulder.

"We'll have to go to the grocery store." Which reminded me of our fateful— fated?—encounter at the Super Saver a couple of weeks ago...

The island's one and only market was a small independent grocery with wooden floors and a limited selection of merchandise. Fortunately, Hershey's bars and marshmallows were not considered exotic fare. Ditto for hot dogs and buns.

I bustled around making responsible selections while Charlie kept piling treats in the cart—tortilla chips, salsa, doughnuts, Frosted Flakes.

I held up the cereal box. "Frosted Flakes?"

"It isn't a proper breakfast without a bowlful of crunchies," he assured me, tossing back the box.

"Are you positive you're a pediatrician?" I asked. "You have deplorable eating habits."

He gave me a sheepish grin, and that's when my tummy did a rhumba. I loved him and I had always loved him. So the question was, should I grab happiness with both hands and damn the consequences, or should I tread carefully? I was afraid that if I didn't leap at this opportunity, I'd never have another chance. However, if I did and our love withered away, I'd be stuck with a Humpty Dumpty heart.

What should I do?

True to his word, Charlie managed to find enough wood to make a bonfire. We even had a gnarled log to lean against, and that was a rarity on this long stretch of unbroken sand. As the blaze crackled and sparks skittered down the beach, we pigged out on hot dogs, marshmallows, potato chips and another bottle of chardonnay. Just when I thought things couldn't get any better, Charlie pulled me back against his chest.

My eyes were watering from the brisk wind whipping off the water, but I could ignore that minor discomfort for this wonderful feeling.

"What would you say to us getting naked in the hot tub?" he whispered.

That would be better than a picnic.

"The hot tub's out on the deck," I said in a sultry voice. "You want me to take my clothes off in public?" It sounded like me, but it really couldn't be, could it? Surely I was having an erotic out-of-body experience. And when I did a sexy wiggle, I was certain I was possessed.

Charlie threw the remnants of our picnic in the hamper. "You can start off in a bathing suit if you insist. I won't guarantee anything after that." Charlie moved his eyebrows suggestively. Then he sprinted to the house. There was something to be said for an impatient man!

The rhythmic surge of the waves was almost enough to lull a girl into complacency. Contentment, however, was not on my menu of feelings tonight. Nope, I was leaning more toward anxiety and terror—especially when I glanced at my butt in the full-length mirror. That's why sarongs were invented. As the old saying has it, nothing ventured, nothing gained. And I planned to gain a lot over the weekend—like an end to my self-imposed celibacy.

"Put me out of my misery and tell me you don't have anything on under that thing," Charlie demanded. Only someone cheeky and charming could get by with that kind of comment.

And speaking of cheeky, someone—I suppose that was me—handed him one end of the sarong.

"Start unwinding and you might be surprised at what you find."

Charlie grinned as he pulled me into the

tub and proceeded to plant hot, wet kisses up my neck and across my jaw to the corner of my mouth. I moved closer and he became the center of my universe. His body was rubbing against mine and his mouth was everywhere, on my breasts, my thighs, my stomach—everywhere. When it became more than I could handle, I took control and straddled his hips.

Charlie's chest was broad and lightly covered with gilded hair. The thought of running my fingers across it sent me into a sensuous kind of ecstasy. This was far beyond sex. I'd never experienced anything like it with Dom.

It was luscious.

It was erotic.

It was better than chocolate!

Chapter 29

That weekend was everything I'd ever wanted, and more. Therein lay the problem. Was I ready for more?

Making life decisions was hard. It seemed that every time I turned around, I encountered a new one. For instance, should Rayna and I make a new life in Meadow Lake? Did I really want to give up my profession and follow my creative side? And the biggest one of all—could I have a future with Charlie?

Divorcing Dom had been a no-brainer. Same for selling the business. I'd always thought of myself as an analytical person, but this had me veering from one emotion to another.

Should I stay or should I go? Ta-ta, dum-da, ta-ta, dum. The lyrics were running in a constant loop through my head. I hated it when an advertising ditty took up residence in my head, and this was *much* worse than a commercial for steel-belted radials.

Meditation was the key to my conundrum, I decided, and what better place to solve a puzzle than out on the dock with a cold lemonade. I hadn't been there five minutes when I was interrupted.

"Hey, girl! I heard from a reliable source that you spent the weekend down at the coast." In a single motion, Misty plopped down on the other deck chair and helped herself to my lemonade. Only a good friend could get away with that type of thievery. "Was Dr. Delicious as delectable as he looks?" She accompanied her comment with a smirk.

I pushed my sunglasses to the top of my head and graced her with one of my best "don't make me mad" scowls. Too bad it was a wasted effort.

"I will not answer that."

"So he was." She broke into gales of laughter. "That's fantastic!"

Fantastic? I wasn't so sure. Especially since just thinking about Charlie turned my brain to mush. My decision had to be analytical and rational.

Didn't it?

Misty, like so many attorneys, was impossible to divert once she focused on a particular topic. Nevertheless, it was worth a try.

"Did you drive down alone or did Bill and Colin come with you?" Misty was the newly elected Attorney General of Texas, so she didn't stray far from Austin.

"Tsk, tsk. Miz Rinaldi, you know better than to try to change the subject. And your love life is exactly what I want to discuss."

Well, darn. "That's too bad. Are you enjoying *my* lemonade?" When in doubt, resort to sarcasm.

"Touché." She gave a fake salute with my glass. "To answer your question, yes, the whole family is here. My mother requested our presence for the weekend, so we decided to stay a couple of extra days."

Not unexpectedly—or not entirely so—Misty and Bill had tied the knot a couple of years after our twentieth reunion. From all accounts, they were very happy.

"Mom, Mom!" Rayna screeched as she barreled toward the dock. Misty's son, Colin, a redheaded devil of fourteen, was chasing her with a water hose. What was the big deal? Rayna spent ninety percent of her time in the water.

"Colin." Misty started to admonish her wayward progeny but was cut short when the teenagers' race across the deck terminated in matching cannonballs. Needless to say, they drenched us. Not that it really mattered. The cool water felt good.

"Gotcha," Colin crowed when he came up for air.

"So you did," Misty said, wiping the moisture from her face. "That brings me to my mission. I was sent over to invite you and Rayna to my parents' house for a picnic this afternoon."

She'd perfected that beseeching look in high school. I'm sure it came in useful during law school, too.

"Say yes. The whole gang will be there," she continued. "Charlie and Alex have confirmed. Plus, Petey and Mary Alice and a couple of their girls are coming. I don't remember which kids. Those flower names confuse me."

I pretended to ponder the invitation. "Yes, we'd love to accept your invitation. What would you like me to bring?"

"We're gonna make this easy. I'll buy some buckets of KFC and if you want to fix a salad, that would be great."

An afternoon of fun and sun with old friends was the perfect way to spend a Sunday. In fact, a permanent move to Texas was becoming more and more appealing.

Charlie shooed one of the kids out of the adjacent lawn chair and sat down beside me—then picked up my hand and kissed my palm.

It was enough to fry a girl's circuits. "Fine." My remark was brief, but at least it wasn't a grunt. Charlie responded with a chuckle.

Summer in Meadow Lake was when people enjoyed life on the river. It was like a perpetual vacation with sunny days, often cool nights, picnics, boating and friends.

"Hey." Billy Tom, aka Bill, sank down on the grass. "I thought we'd take the kids inner tubing. You guys okay with that?" Bill addressed the group in general; however, the kids answered, and you can imagine their response.

Bill, Petey, Rayna, Alex, Colin and Dahlia piled into one boat. They were planning to do the strenuous stuff. The passengers on the parent vessel—including Charlie, Misty, Mary Alice and, of course, me—were content to drop anchor and simply enjoy the afternoon.

Even at the ripe old age of fifty-something, Charlie looked just fine in his swim trunks. I wish I could say the same about my body. Some of the bits and pieces had settled in slightly different places. Thank goodness Charlie didn't seem to notice. In fact, he was quite appreciative....

I was immersed in a rather erotic day-dream when things went awry. We were anchored in the middle of the river, minding our own business and watching our kids, when a powerboat carrying two drunk Bubbas almost rammed us.

"Watch where you're going!" Charlie yelled, although I'm not sure they heard him.

"That is so stupid! Don't those idiots know they can get killed pulling that crap?" Misty shook her fist at the boat as it sped off.

Boating while drunk was incredibly stupid and dangerous. "They're gone, let's forget it," I said, primarily to placate Misty, who was practically frothing at the mouth.

"All right, but it makes me furious."

"Do you guys want a drink?" Mary Alice was still practicing the art of changing the subject. "Is a Diet Coke okay?" She reached into the ice chest containing soft drinks.

"I'll take one," I answered.

"Me, too." Misty grinned. "I need to lighten up, right?"

"Right," Mary Alice and I said in unison, then we broke into giggles.

"Petey is like an overgrown kid." Mary Alice sent her husband a loving look. Petey and Colin were holding on to inner tubes while Bill pulled them through the water. Everyone was having fun, laughing.

Misty started to say something but was interrupted by the roar of an engine. The Bubbas were back.

"Oh, my God!" Mary Alice screamed. "They're heading straight for the kids!" Her screech turned into a high keening noise.

From that point on, the whole fiasco seemed to play out in slow motion. I couldn't, or maybe wouldn't, process the disaster my brain told me was about to happen. It felt like the accident back in 1973. Not again! Please not again! Not with my baby here.

I was snapped out of my stupor by a horrendous crash, followed by a scream that would haunt me until the day I died.

Misty grabbed me, pointing mutely toward the carnage. She was shaking so hard I thought we'd both fall overboard.

I couldn't believe what I was seeing. The speedboat had come to rest on the hull of Bill's vessel. It looked almost like some macabre mating ritual.

"Oh, my God, oh, my God, oh, my God," Mary Alice repeated over and over as she collapsed on the cushion.

"Call nine-one-one," Charlie yelled, slamming his cell phone into my hand. A second later, he was in the water swimming toward the wreckage.

My kid was out there!

"Mary Alice, Mary Alice!" I made sure I had her attention before I handed her the phone. "Call nine-one-one. And stay in the boat until they get here. Misty, come with me." With my baby out there, I didn't have the luxury of breaking down.

By then Misty had come to her senses and was in the water. I dived in after her.

With all the adrenaline pulsing through my system I'm sure I broke a couple of Olympic records. We were at least fifty yards from the accident and I don't think it took us more than a few minutes to get to the wreckage. That was a gold-medal swim by anyone's standard, and Charlie was even faster than we were.

He was on Bill's boat making a quick assessment of the situation by the time Misty and I reached our destination.

I was praying for a miracle but expecting the worst.

"Rayna! Rayna!" I screamed. I was a hysterical mess. Who could blame me? That was my *baby* out there. My baby. And I was well acquainted with the fact that people *died* in boating accidents. It had happened before.

Charlie shook me, none too gently. "Jasmine. Jasmine. They're. Not. On. The. Boat. Check the water. Do you understand me?"

I nodded.

"This guy's going to bleed to death if I don't help him immediately." He was referring to the drunk who was hemorrhaging— the man I planned to pummel if he actually made it out of this alive.

It took a few seconds for Charlie's words to sink in. The kids were in the water. They had personal flotation devices. Please God, they'd be okay.

"I see a couple of people over there." Misty pointed downriver.

I shaded my eyes with my hand. "It's Petey and Colin," I yelled, jumping up and down like a crazy person. "They're still on the inner tube."

When Petey waved to indicate they were okay, Misty almost fainted in relief.

"We'll swim over to Charlie's boat. Find everyone else," Petey called.

He didn't have to tell me twice. *Rayna was missing.* I scanned the water so frantically it felt like my head was on a swivel. Finally, I saw two more bright-yellow life vests.

"There, over there!" I pointed at two people bobbing in the water.

"Who is it?" I was leaning so far over the edge I almost tumbled into the river.

"They're, uh, I think, uh…" Misty turned toward Charlie, who was creating a make-shift tourniquet. "Charlie! Alex and Dahlia are out there. They look okay."

"Thank God." He sagged in relief as he continued to administer first aid.

Petey, Dahlia, Colin and Alex were alive

and accounted for. That meant Bill and Rayna were missing. Please, please, *please,* let them be okay. I was about to make God all kinds of offers when I heard Rayna's voice.

"Mama. Mama!"

I scrambled to the other side of the boat and there she was in the water—the most beautiful sight in the world. Rayna. Wet. Scared out of her mind. And alive!

"Bill," Misty screamed, and immediately leaped into the river to join her husband.

"Bill!" Charlie yelled. He was in full E.R. mode. "I need your help. And Jazzy, round up everyone and swim over to my boat. This thing—" he knocked on the hull of the Bubbas' boat "—is leaking gas. I'm afraid it might blow."

Good God! What next?

"Come with us, please," I implored, although I knew he wouldn't leave his patient.

"I can't." He shook his head. "I've done all I can for this guy but there's another victim here somewhere. We have to find him and get him off this boat."

"Okay," I reluctantly agreed and jumped

into the water with Misty, who was as distraught as I felt.

"Come on." I tugged on Misty's bathing suit strap. "Let's get the kids to safety. Then we'll figure everything out." I don't know whether I was trying to assure her or me.

Although I was feeling strangely calm, I knew from my previous experience that when the adrenaline ran out, I'd crash and burn like the Hindenburg.

"Rayna, swim over to Mary Alice. Can you get there?" Misty yelled. My daughter looked shell-shocked, but she nodded.

Good old Misty. She'd slipped into her take-charge lawyer persona and was halfway to Dahlia and Colin before I had Rayna headed in the right direction. Now I had to see if I could help the guys.

The smell of gasoline was overpowering. That piece of junk was leaking like a sieve. Swim. Faster! *Charlie needs help.* I was so focused on returning to the boat I almost missed the roar of another engine. It was the sound of salvation.

"Back off! We have a leak," Charlie

yelled at the two men in a Bayliner who'd pulled up to the wreckage.

The driver obviously got the drift. Before you could blink an eye, he hit Reverse and backed up thirty or forty feet. It was far enough to get out of the range of a fireball. His passenger, however, hit the water and did an Australian crawl straight into an imminent calamity.

What would we do without heroes?

"Here." His friend's boat appeared next to where I was treading water. He extended a hand. "Don't worry. My buddy's a fireman. He loves to pull people out of tough situations." His grin made me feel a lot better.

And sure enough, he was right. Praise the Lord and pass the ammunition—he was right.

Minutes after the sheriff's water patrol arrived and everyone was evacuated, including the two Bubbas, both boats burned to the waterline. Bill was more than a little annoyed, and who could blame him? That vessel was his pride and joy.

Chapter 30

As far as disasters went, yesterday's debacle was a doozy. With the resiliency of youth, Rayna sprang back immediately. I suppose it helped that I was able to locate Dom so she could be consoled by her dad. I, on the other hand, wasn't capable of much more than sitting around moaning.

Well, I wasn't exactly moaning, although I did feel like a hundred and twenty pounds of doggie doo. Until my cell phone chirped. "Hello," I said hopefully.

"Hey, Sunshine." Oh, yeah. It was Charlie. "Good news. The guy with the bad cut's going to make it, and the other one was released from the hospital today."

"Did the cops cite them for drunken boating?"

"Yep."

I could feel his grin through the phone lines.

"They could've killed someone."

"I was afraid they had." This time his tone was serious.

"So was I."

"Your mom invited the Morrison guys to dinner."

"She did?"

"You didn't know?"

"No, but that's great. I've been in a blue funk and it's her way of cheering me up. It'll be good for the kids to get together. How's Alex doing? He's such a sweetie."

"Pretty well. My mom's spoiling him rotten. So far she's made him a cake *and* a pie."

"The same thing's happening here. Mama's in a baking frenzy."

"So you're feeling depressed, huh?" he asked, moving on from the subject of sugar therapy.

"Uh-huh. The whole episode reminds me of that accident in the summer of '73, when Stuart died. Do you remember how I fell apart?"

"You were fine that time, and you will be now," he assured me. "Will seeing me cheer you up?"

"Definitely!"

Mama, bless her pea-pickin' heart, was matchmaking again. She hadn't missed an opportunity to throw us together. Impromptu suppers at home and family get-togethers at the Catfish Shack—whatever it took, she was willing to do it. Generally, it involved food. Lord in heaven, if she didn't quit soon, my butt would—well, let me remind you of that barn door.

I'm sure she had visions of a new grandson to spoil. But she didn't have to work that hard. Charlie and I were destined to be together. The only thing I hadn't quite figured out was the logistics.

"If you're feeling any ill effects from yesterday, I can bring over my bag and we can play doctor."

As sexy offers went, that was really, *really* tempting.

"Uh-huh," I answered. And then I had the great awakening. We didn't have any privacy. *Any* privacy! That was a problem. The great outdoors was risky, and a car? Hey, at our age we wouldn't live through *that* experience. Plus, prudish though it might seem, Mama's house was verboten. Alex was at Charlie's, and much as I adored him, having a child around when grown-ups wanted privacy was difficult.

Remember the comic-book lightbulb effect? Well, that was how I suddenly felt. I loved Charlie, and come hell or high water, I was going to make him a permanent part of my life. To do that, Rayna and I had to become residents of the great state of Texas. It was simple!

Yippee, yi, yo, ki, ya—or something like that.

I was right about Mama and Rayna; they were engaged in baking therapy, and the kitchen smelled like chocolate. Yummy, yummy chocolate—God's gift to happiness.

"Hi, Mom," Rayna said. She was wearing a huge grin and a big brown smear on her cheek. "We made brownies, and cookies and a cake."

Mama glanced at me, barely suppressing a grimace. Baking was Mama's signature way of relieving stress, and wow, her stress meter had to be off the charts. Although she was putting on a brave face, I knew what she was thinking. Rayna had come very close to being killed. I'm not sure either of us would have survived that.

"Rayna, sweetie. Would you sit down? I want to talk to you."

I could tell she was about to whine, then she reconsidered and plopped herself in the chair.

"You like it here, don't you?" I began.

"Yeah, I guess."

All that enthusiasm was wonderful.

"And you like it here at Grammy's house?"

I knew the exact moment she realized where the conversation was going. I also knew she was happy, but Rayna, of course, wouldn't make this easy.

"Hmm," she answered with a nonchalant shrug.

"I've decided we should move here. I want to keep this house in the family." I continued my explanation without allowing her an opportunity to protest. "You already know some kids so it won't be hard to make a school change. And I want the Morrisons to be part of our family. You like Charlie and Alex, so that'll be good. And you can go see your dad anytime you want." Dom hadn't remarried, and although he traveled extensively he always made time for Rayna.

Considering that Charlie had never mentioned marriage, I wasn't sure what he'd think of my idea. But I suspected he'd give it a big thumbs-up.

I was expecting a full-blown "you're ruining my life" diatribe. Darn it, if she didn't totally shock me with her response.

"Okay. That's cool."

I wasn't often rendered speechless, but my thirteen-year-old had managed it.

"That's cool?" I repeated.

"Yeah. Dahlia and I want to go shopping.

She said she saw this sundress at Target. You have to drive us. Please?"

"I can do that." Would someone please wake me? I tell her we're about to turn our lives topsy-turvy, and she casually changes the discussion to a sundress.

"Cool. I'm gonna get some sun." She grabbed a couple of cookies before she scooted off to put on her bathing suit.

Mama took the seat Rayna had vacated. "Are you really going to buy my house?"

"Yes, ma'am."

"And are you serious about Charlie and Alex?"

"Yes."

She gave me a huge hug. "I'm glad. You know I think the world of Charlie and Alex. In my opinion, this is absolutely wonderful for everyone concerned."

Normally I wouldn't consider discussing my love life, or lack of one, with my mother. This time, however, I decided she might have some genuine insight.

"So you really like Charlie," I said.

She didn't hesitate a second. "I think he's perfect for you."

"When I was a teenager, you didn't think that."

Mama patted my hand. "Your daddy and I were wrong. The climate was different then. There were ironclad rules about social class." She shrugged. "I realize now that we were following the crowd. Believe me, your daddy and I regretted what we did. I'm glad he had the opportunity to apologize to Charlie."

I could feel my eyes fill with tears.

"So have a brownie and go call Charlie. He'll be pleased as punch." She slid the plate of goodies over in front of me. "On second thought, have a bunch of brownies. You need the endorphins."

Would wonders never cease? Mama was talking about endorphins.

Marvelous news should be delivered in person, not on the phone. So I decided to wait until dinner to tell Charlie about my decision. I hoped he'd be as excited as I was. I thought he would be, but what I knew about the workings of the male mind would fill a small teacup.

"Mom, phone for you," Rayna called. She was dressed and ready for our shopping expedition. "Don't talk forever," she whined, handing me the cordless.

I prayed I'd live through the whining phase without throttling her. Because if I *did* throttle her, I'd have to surrender my good-mother badge.

"Hello," I said, expecting either Charlie or Mary Alice. Was I ever wrong.

"Hi, Jazzy. It's Bunny."

Knock me over with a feather.

"I'm in town and I hoped we could go out for lunch."

"Yeah, um, okay." What else could I say? My first instinct was to make an excuse, but my manners made a surprise appearance. I hadn't talked to Bunny since that fiasco at the reunion.

"Great," she said, and sounded as if she meant it. "Does noon tomorrow at Sally's Tearoom work for you?"

What in the world did we have in common anymore? Nothing. "That's fine. Hey, listen. Rayna's waiting for me to take her to Target, so I've got to run. I'll see you to-morrow."

That left me with an entire day to wonder why Bunny was home and what she wanted. And by the way, how did she know I was in Meadow Lake?

All during our dinner with the Morrison men, Mama wore a smirk. It was as if she had a delightful secret and was dying to share it. Although I gave her the glare, it had about as much impact on her as it did on Rayna.

Meanwhile, Alex was ragging on Rayna like a pesky little brother. But everything considered, they seemed to be pals.

"Why don't you take Alex up to your room? You guys can play your Xbox."

"Cool," Alex responded.

Ninety-five percent of the time, Rayna was pure teenage girl—clothes, hair, makeup, the whole enchilada. The other five percent she turned into an all-American tomboy. Fortunately, this was one of those times.

"Come on," she commanded. "I have this great game where everybody has an MP-5."

That got Alex's attention.

"What's an MP-5?" Mama asked.

"A gun," I replied, even though I was way out of my league on that subject.

"What kind of gun?"

"One that shoots bullets."

Mama did that tsking thing of hers that drives me nuts. "Have you—"

"Don't go there."

The woman was dying to know if I'd talked to Charlie.

Smart man that he was, Charlie stayed quiet throughout the entire conversation.

We strolled down to the dock hand in hand. He was obviously entertaining lascivious thoughts, and it seemed a shame to put a damper on all that lust—a damned shame.

I waited until we were cuddled on a chaise before I dropped my conversational bomb.

"Bunny called this afternoon."

It took him a moment to realize what I'd said. "Did you say *Bunny?*"

"None other."

"She's in town?"

"Oh, yes."

"What did she want?"

I gave him a smile that I hoped would curl *his* toes. "She's in town, and she wants to meet me for lunch."

"Really?"

"Uh-huh."

"I trust we're not going to have all that drama again."

Amen to that, brother, amen!

"Let's change the subject," I suggested, mentally preparing for my big announcement. Please God, this was the right time and place. "I made a decision."

"Oh?" Charlie was dropping soft kisses from my ear to the corner of my mouth. It was hard to think—much less carry on a cogent conversation—when he did *that*.

Focus, girl, focus. "I've decided to buy Mama's house."

He sat up so fast I almost fell off the deck chair. "You're doing what?"

Talk about an *interesting* reaction. I wasn't quite sure it was good feedback, but it was noteworthy. "Rayna and I are making a permanent move to Meadow Lake."

"Are you serious?"

"Absolutely."

"Hot damn!" He pumped a fist in the air.

Now, that was a response I could appreciate.

Chapter 31

I was a chicken—yep, a 100 percent feather-bearing fowl. That's why I coerced Mary Alice into accompanying me to the tearoom. There was safety in numbers and when dealing with Bunny, safety seemed like a wise move.

"I can't believe I agreed to this," M.A. complained.

At least she wasn't squealing. In my present state of mind I couldn't have handled that.

"She's your friend, too. So get a grip."

Sally's Tearoom had typical girly cuisine—you know the drill—scones, fluffy salads decorated with strawberries and candied pecans, thimble-sized sandwiches and tiny bowls of soup. Not a whiff of chocolate, and I needed some processed sugar for *this* meeting.

Mary Alice must've been reading my mind.

"We should've stopped at Candy Land and picked up some fudge," she muttered. "I think we're gonna need it."

"Absolutely."

"That must be Bunny." Mary Alice indicated the blonde in a Mercedes who'd pulled into the parking lot.

Leave it to Bunny to drive the only luxury German car in a parking lot full of Suburbans and American-made sedans.

"What do you suppose her deal is?" M.A. asked.

"Guess we'll find out in a minute." I suppressed the urge to cross myself. Since I wasn't Catholic, it wouldn't do me a bit of good.

Although a clove of garlic might not be a bad idea. I'd figured out in retrospect that

Bunny was a psychic vampire. I'd read a magazine article about "toxic friendships," and that described Bunny perfectly. She was one of those people who, if you let them, sucked the life right out of you. It wasn't intentional or malicious, it was just Bunny.

"Oh, wow," Mary Alice mumbled.

And *oh, wow* barely covered my reaction. Bunny hadn't aged well. She was coiffed and dressed beautifully, but there was a hard edge that even the finest designer couldn't disguise. What had happened to her?

I stood to get her attention. "Bunny, we're over here."

A smile brightened her face. Somehow, I instinctively knew that smiles were a rare commodity in her life.

"Jazz." I could tell that she was ready to launch into her big-city-girl act, but I circumvented the air kiss and hugged her for all I was worth. She stiffened momentarily, and although she didn't quite reciprocate the affection, she didn't push me away. As far as I was concerned, that equated to one point for our team.

Yay!

Mary Alice looked at me before she embraced our old friend. "I'm glad you're here."

"So am I," Bunny agreed before sitting down.

"Let's decide what we want to eat and then you—" Mary Alice pointed at Bunny "—better fess up on what's happening."

I did a double take. As far as I knew, Mary Alice hadn't jumped on anyone like that since the day she took me to task.

After we were served our salads, we got down to the business of being old friends. Despite the ups and downs and trials and tribulations of the years, despite Bunny's poor track record as a friend, we were rekindling a bond that had been forged when we were learning how to jump rope.

"You look like you haven't slept in a year."

Go get 'em, Mary Alice!

Bunny grimaced. "Yeah, well. Life hasn't been a walk in the park."

"Give," Mary Alice insisted.

Since the Mistress of the Inquisition was

going full blast, I didn't have to do anything but sit back and watch the action.

"My husband, or should I say my estranged husband, was snagged by the SEC for insider trading. Unfortunately, his shenanigans got him sent to a country-club prison and left me virtually destitute." She shrugged. "So I came back to the nest."

That was worse than my sob story.

"Here I am." Bunny spread her arms as if to encompass the entire world. "I have no job experience and no way to make a living. I own a closet full of beautiful clothes and this." She held up her hand, displaying a diamond the size of a small quail egg. "Know anyone who wants to buy a ten-carat perfect yellow diamond? I'll make them the deal of a lifetime."

Yeah, sure. Didn't everyone know a "fence"?

"Oh, Bunny. That's awful." I couldn't resist giving her another hug. The least I could do was tell her my story. It might make her feel better.

"I brought my teenage daughter to Meadow Lake to test the idea of going home again. The jury just brought in a good-to-go verdict." I had to laugh; the jury I was referring to was my thirteen-year-old daughter.

"So you're divorced."

"I sure am." Dom had been a bad husband but he was a reasonably good dad, and he wasn't doing time.

My ruminations were cut short by Mary Alice's next question.

"Do you have any experience in retail?"

Bunny gave her the same look I'm sure was on my face. What did that have to do with the price of tea in China?

"Um, what do you mean by retail? If you're talking about credit cards I'm the queen of plastic."

"Actually, I've been thinking about introducing a more expensive line of clothing. You might be the perfect person to sell it." Mary Alice eyed Bunny's outfit. It was obviously couture.

"Me?" Bunny put her hand on her chest. "Work for *you*?" She pointed at Mary Alice.

Uh-oh. Here's where the excrement hit the fan.

"Yes." Somehow Mary Alice turned it into three or four syllables.

"Are you kidding?"

"No. I'm dead serious."

"Oh, my God, I'd love to!"

"You would?"

"Absolutely! Do you realize this would be my first paying job since I worked those two weeks at the Dairy Queen when we were juniors?"

"Um, well, um." Mary Alice waved her hand in an indecipherable gesture. "Don't you worry, not for a minute. You're home now and things will work out, just you wait and see. We're friends, and friends help each other."

Mary Alice's comment reminded me of what I had to do—stake my claim on Charlie.

"Before we get into a group hug, there's something I have to say."

My statement was enough to temporarily derail their discussion of new clothing lines.

"Just for the record, Charlie's mine." I was shocked at how easily those words tripped off my tongue.

Bunny looked startled for a moment, then she broke into laughter. "So that's how it is."

"That's how it is."

"Good, I'm glad. You two are great together. You always have been."

Was Bunny really giving me her blessing? Wow!

Chapter 32

Sometimes things didn't turn out the way you expected. I'd dreaded lunch and it was an incredible validation of friendship. It wasn't as if we could turn back the clock, or forget everything that had happened in the intervening years. However, some relationships could be sustained despite it all.

"I wish Misty was here," Bunny commented right before they kicked us out of the tearoom.

Who could blame them? We'd stayed well beyond their closing hour and I'm sure we were annoying them with our raucous laughter. You would've thought we were downing margaritas instead of Earl Grey.

We were standing in the parking lot discussing our next get-together when Mary Alice whipped out her cell phone.

"I'll call Misty and tell her to come down this weekend. We'll have a party at my house."

"I have to go home and check on Rayna." I dug my keys out of the bottom of my purse. "Let me know when and what I need to bring." I gave Bunny a hug. "I'm so glad we had lunch."

"So am I."

We were dangerously close to a flood of tears, so it was time to beat feet.

"Call me," I said before I scurried off to my car.

"Rayna! Mama!" I wandered through the kitchen on my way to the living room. The house was very quiet—no country music on the radio, no hip-hop from upstairs, just blessed silence. Mama's car was gone, so it was a good bet Rayna had conned her grandma into a shopping trip.

Oh, to be an only grandchild. But not for long!

I was wearing a sappy smile as I picked up the stack of mail. My grin lasted until I saw the official, fat, odious envelope bearing the return address of a San Francisco law firm.

Almost any letter from an attorney was not a good thing. And boy, oh, boy, I didn't know the half of it.

By the time I finished reading the entire missive, steam was rolling out of my ears.

Dom, Dom, Dom! How could he?

What had I just been thinking? Oh, right. That my ex was a terrible husband, but at least he was an okay father. Was I the stupidest person on the planet?

I crumpled the letter. What a load of crap! Dom claimed that the environment I was providing for Rayna wasn't safe and he was going back to court to get custody.

Can you say homicidal? The man ran around on me. How *dare* he say I'm not a good mother! Everything I'd done in the past thirteen years was in Rayna's best interests. All I wanted was five minutes with that sucker and he'd be sorry.

When my white-hot rage subsided, and I'd somehow gathered my wits, I called Charlie. Fortunately he was between patients and answered immediately.

He didn't say a thing while I dumped my problems in his lap. And, believe me, I went with the whole routine—sobs, hiccups and graphic expletives.

"Don't worry."

"But—"

"I'll talk to Colton and call you right back."

"Colton?"

"My brother, remember?"

"Of course I know Colton. Why are you calling him?"

"Because he's a family attorney and he specializes in custody issues."

"Okay." Another annoying hiccup.

"I'll come out as soon as I see my last patient. Go take a nice hot bath and, sweetheart, don't worry. We'll get this sorted out."

I certainly hoped so. If I killed Dom—as

I felt inclined to do—I'd be wearing an orange jumpsuit for the rest of my life.

I'm not quite sure how I made it through the day. I was determined to keep my family in the dark, so I did my best Miss America impression—complete with a big smile, a hair toss and a giggle.

When Charlie arrived bearing a huge bouquet of daisies and roses, I was tempted to toss him to the ground and ravish him. What a sweet man. If he could salvage this I'd nominate him for sainthood.

"Hey, Sunshine. How are you doing?" he asked, leading me down to the dock.

"Other than the fact that I'm about to hyperventilate, I'm okay."

"Let's sit down." He made himself at home on a chaise and pulled me into his lap.

That was more like it!

The only reason we came up for air was that a boat full of teenagers roared by hooting and hollering.

"They're jealous," Charlie said, continuing to nibble on my neck.

"Uh-huh." He could stop what he was doing in, say, thirty minutes.

"So," he said as he readjusted me on his lap to put some distance between us, "Colton said he'll come down on Saturday. He suggests you invite Dom here for a talk. If he's reasonable, he'll see that Rayna's perfectly safe. I suspect he's reacting to his fear after the boating accident."

"You might be right," I conceded.

"Is he a levelheaded kind of guy?"

"Sometimes. Honestly, I have no idea what he'll do. I never thought he'd cheat on me."

"What do you think about talking this out with him?"

I took only a second to make my decision. If we could solve this problem without going to court, we'd all be better off.

"Okay, I'll call him," I said. "Rayna will be glad to see him." Even if I wouldn't.

Two days later, I was at the San Antonio airport picking up my ex-husband. He'd never enjoyed our trips to Texas, so I'm sure he considered this quite an imposition.

"Why didn't Rayna come with you?" We were standing at the carousel in baggage claim trying to be congenial. So far, our temporary truce was working.

"She's water-skiing with a neighbor kid."

"You let her do that without adult supervision?"

He probably meant it as a reasonable question, but it felt like another indictment of my maternal skills. Snapping at him was not the right approach, so I took a deep, soothing breath. I hoped that would calm my spiking blood pressure.

"Mother's at home and her friend Cissy's dad is driving the boat." I didn't tell him I was still having nightmares about the accident. Or the fact that sometimes the catastrophe with Stuart would bleed over into my memories of the latest incident. That information was strictly on a need-to-know basis, and he'd forfeited any right to my innermost secrets.

We were being so formal it made my teeth hurt. What had happened to us? We'd been married. We were business partners. Now we could barely carry on a conversation.

"You certainly don't have the congestion problem we have in California." He was referring to the light traffic on Interstate 10. He was right. When I first returned to Texas, I had culture shock. The pace was much slower than in the Bay Area, and although I'd spent most of my adult life in California, I knew I couldn't go back.

California wasn't my home, not really. Perhaps home was more of a state of mind, or a person, than an actual place. And that made me think of Charlie.

"I made you a reservation at the Holiday Inn, but you're certainly welcome to stay in Mother's guest room."

"The motel will be fine." I wasn't surprised. Dom and my parents had never been close, and this situation wasn't going to help matters.

"I'd also like to rent a car. I don't want to impose on you."

"Of course. When we get to town, I'll take you to the rental place." This stilted conversation was making me crazy, and I couldn't wait to get back to Meadow Lake. Even if his visit only lasted two days, it would be the longest two days of my life.

Thirty minutes later, we were in the parking lot of the Enterprise office. "Do you remember how to get to the river house?"

"I think I can find it." His comments were painfully succinct. If our communication went on in that vein, solving our custody problem through negotiation would be impossible.

"We're expecting you for dinner. Rayna's anxious to see you. Why don't you come over around six?"

He nodded and started to get out of the car.

"Wait." I surprised myself with that command.

He closed the car door, waiting for me to say whatever I intended to say.

"Look, Dom. Let's stop acting like we're on a bad blind date and discuss Rayna." I was ready to beg.

"I don't want to commit to anything until I talk to my daughter." On that rather discouraging note, he got out of the car and walked into the rental office.

Well, hell!

Chapter 33

Dom was a stranger. He couldn't be the person I'd married and promised to love until I died. Granted, I'd never felt for him what I did for Charlie, but I thought we'd developed mutual affection, as well as respect. What in the world had happened to us? My skin was clammy and I felt like I was about to throw up. I had misjudged my husband on almost all levels—his ability to be faithful, his commitment to our business partnership and, most importantly, his concern for Rayna. Was he honestly worried about his daughter or—as I suspected—was he trying to get back at me?

And that brought me to another question. If I could misjudge a man I'd spent decades with, both professionally and personally, how could I be sure about Charlie?

All I wanted to do was jump into bed, pull up the covers and worry about it tomorrow, but that wasn't an option. Dom was coming to dinner.

I was the mother of his child and he was treating me like someone he'd barely met!

If he'd changed that much, how could I believe Charlie would be any different? And if that was the case, how could I consider building a life with him?

But I loved Charlie, I reminded myself, and he loved me. That was the difference.

"Hey, Sunshine." Charlie was standing next to his car when I pulled into the driveway.

Charlie was strong. He was safe, now and forever.

My doubts evaporated like mist in the sunshine.

Not that I'm big on necking in driveways, but I was desperate for a kiss. So I drew his head down and shamelessly went for it. After my Dom encounter, I needed reassurance that the world was still on its proper axis.

Charlie tunneled his fingers through my hair. "Did you take him to the motel, or did you kill him on the way?"

"I killed him and dumped his body off I-10. If I'm lucky, it won't make the news."

Grinning, he shook his head, then lowered his face for another kiss. "Let's go out to the dam so we can have a nice private discussion." He tugged my hand, leading me toward his car.

"To talk?"

His suggestive chuckle sent a jolt of electricity straight up my spine. And I knew.

He wasn't Dom. He'd never be Dom. I could trust Charlie with my life, my heart and my future.

I couldn't wait to get my hands on him, and apparently the sentiment was mutual. We walked to the edge of the water and

found our special place. It provided a bit
of privacy in a busy world. Charlie was the
only man who'd ever rendered me senseless
with a simple embrace. We had wasted so
many years, and I wasn't willing to squan-
der one minute more.

As we sat on the grass, Charlie took me in
his embrace. If I'd been in a rational state of
mind, this would be when I'd be singing hal-
lelujah. My guardian angel was on the job
and she'd brought me to the love of my life.

It *was* possible to go home again. And
Charlie was my home.

Seclusion was good. Was it ever! Charlie
was a man with a slow hand, and he opened
the buttons of my blouse, inch by agonizing inch.

When he'd finally accomplished his goal,
the warm summer air soothed my over-
heated skin. The respite didn't last long.
When he started suckling my breasts, my
temperature spiked and all thought was lost
in a haze of longing.

"Marry me. We can apply for a license
and have a ceremony in a couple of days."

"Hmm." I was too busy playing with the crinkly hair on his chest to be carrying on a conversation.

"I'm serious. I love you. I always have. Let's get married, the sooner the better."

That was so tempting, but I was still hesitant. "I have to fix this thing with Rayna and Dom. I won't let her move back to California without me." I was terrified; if I had to make a decision, I'd choose my child and then I'd lose Charlie again.

"You're thinking too much. Just let your heart make your decisions." Charlie's comment was punctuated by a series of nibbles beginning at the base of my neck and working up to my ear. "Don't worry. Colton's working on it. And he's as much of a bulldog as I am."

I wasn't positive anything would produce the right results, but for now, I'd just enjoy my time with Charlie. Goose bumps popped up on my arms as he continued to alternately kiss and nibble.

"Do you like that?" he asked.

"Uh-huh."

"If we get married, we can do this all

the time," Charlie murmured, trailing kisses down my stomach.

Darn him—he had a point, and a delicious way of emphasizing it. Still…

What was I thinking? I *loved* him!

"Okay," I muttered.

"What?" Charlie raised his head. He was wearing the cocky grin that never failed to send my heart into an abnormal rhythm.

"I said I'd marry you. I've always loved you, too." I levered myself up on my elbows to see his reaction, not that I really needed to. His whoop could've been heard in the next county.

Who'd believe he was a respected professional and a pillar of the community?

My Charlie.

Chapter 34

"Daddy, did you know that Mom's planning to buy Grammy's house and we're gonna live in Meadow Lake?" Leave it to a child to get right to the heart of the matter.

"Yes, sweetie, I did. What do you think of that?" Dom asked, glancing in my direction.

"It's okay." She did her typical teenage shrug. Somewhere between childhood and adolescence, Rayna had mastered a number of annoying traits.

"Wouldn't you rather go to your old school and see all your old friends?"

She shrugged again. For once, I appreciated her special form of nonverbal communication. Dom, however, wasn't amused. He wanted a quick answer, and he wanted the response that would validate his opinion.

I could tell that my mother was champing at the bit to tell him to get lost. Fortunately, she managed to control her basic grandmotherly instincts.

"More potatoes?" she asked. She was trying to head off Dom's current line of questioning. Hooray for her. I couldn't seem to hold up my end of the conversation. The thought of losing Rayna made me ill.

"No, thank you. The meal was delicious." Dom put down his fork with a clink. That meant he was finished with his meal.

The question was, what did he plan to do next? Was he trying to convince Rayna she'd be happier with him? And could he succeed? Like any mother and daughter, we'd had our rough moments—nothing major, but all bets were off when you're trying to understand the mind of a thirteen-year-old.

"Would you like some dessert?" Mama addressed Dom. She was trying her darnedest to win him over through food. Too bad she was hitting a brick wall.

"No, thank you," he answered again, polite as always but distant. That was his personality.

"Rayna, would you like to go to the mall in San Antonio with me tomorrow?"

He might as well have asked her whether she wanted to breathe.

"Yeah! That'd be sweet. Can I bring a friend?"

Dom looked nonplussed. His tolerance for giggly girls was limited. "I would like to have a day with you alone."

Rayna didn't seem too happy with his reply. "Yeah. Sure. Whatever. Mom, can I go next door? Cissy's got some new magazines we're gonna look at."

Dom was so out of his element it was almost funny.

"That's fine." I waited until she left before I continued.

"Dom and I are going out on the patio, Mama."

"Oh, okay." Mama was obviously relieved to get her ex-son-in-law out of her kitchen, and I couldn't blame her. I wanted him out of Texas. And now, without our two chaperones, we could get down to business.

Talking Dom out of anything he wanted to do wasn't easy. But this time the stakes were too high to fail. Rayna was not moving to California—and neither was I.

"Dom—"

He interrupted before I could start a sentence. "I don't believe she's safe here."

I slammed my coffee cup on the table. Getting mad at him was the wrong thing to do, but I'm only human. I closed my eyes and counted to ten, a very long ten.

"I can't guarantee that nothing will ever happen to her, but neither can you, Dom. She could step off the bus and get hit by a car. That could happen in California. We can't wrap our kids in cotton and expect them to live normal lives."

"I'm trying to look after her best interests."

Although that was debatable, this was not the time to get into it with him. So I tried appealing to his pragmatic side. Although he was an architect, he had the personality of an engineer.

"Okay, look at it this way. You travel all over the world. What would you do with a young girl while you're gone?" I couldn't resist giving him one of my infamous arched eyebrows. He hated that. "Would you leave her with a nanny?"

"No." He sighed, resting his forearms on his thighs. "I hate having this kind of discussion with you." He paused as if trying to decide what to say next.

And that led me to believe he was going to try to win this argument. Little did he know he didn't have a chance.

"Look, Dom." I put my hand on his. "As a couple, we were terrible. That doesn't negate the fact that we were friends for years. Let's talk this out. The last thing you want to do is hurt Rayna. She's happy here. I know she is. And I think you know it, too."

He didn't say a word, so I pressed on.

"I believe with all my heart that this move is the right thing to do. Think about it—she can spend every summer and spring break with you. That way, you can plan to be in

the country at those times, and still not re-
strict your career opportunities."

We'd arrived at the no-nonsense approach
to this problem, and that's where Dom ex-
celled. He was a hard-nosed man who was
also very realistic. I could tell the moment
my argument hit home.

"Are you *sure* she's happy here?"

"Yes. Dom, we're both happy."

"I was afraid of that." He hung his head.
"Jasmine, where did we go wrong?"

I took his other hand. "We didn't love
each other. We never should've gotten married."

"I know." Dom nodded his head in agreement.

I'd never quite realized what the phrase
pregnant silence meant until then. That particular moment was so pregnant it could've
had quadruplets. Then, finally, Dom spoke.

"When I get home, I'll tell my lawyer to
forget about the custody suit. I'm willing to
abide by our current arrangement. But I am
absolutely going to hold you to my visita-
tion rights."

"And well you should. I *want* you to have a relationship with Rayna."

"I do, too." He stood. "I'll head back to the motel now. Tell Rayna I'll pick her up in the morning. We're going on a shopping trip."

I wanted to whoop, holler and kick my heels together; common sense told me to control myself. "I'll tell her. And Dom, I think we've both made a good decision."

"Me, too." The man I'd married and lived with for so many years kissed me on the top of the head. Then he was gone.

Dom was my past. Charlie was my present. I couldn't wait to tell him the news.

There was life, and love, and all kinds of adventure after fifty! And I planned to savor every minute of it with Charlie.

Chapter 35

"Would you stand still? I'm trying to button this thing," Mary Alice said.

I was as nervous as the proverbial cat in a roomful of rocking chairs. I was getting married!

Charlie and I had briefly, very briefly, considered eloping to Las Vegas. Bad idea! Everyone, and I do mean everyone, in Meadow Lake would've been miffed. So here I was with my three best friends while the love of my life was waiting for me.

Mama had bought her condo, and Rayna and I had moved into her house. Charlie and

I had two households to consolidate, two kids to make happy, and two families to placate. Charlie's mom wanted to have the reception at her restaurant and Mama was determined to rent the country club. Those two worlds would never meet. So Charlie and I compromised. We decided to celebrate our wedding with a picnic by the river.

"Charlie wants to see you," Misty said. "He's wearing a goofy grin. I told him no way, it's unlucky."

That's my Misty, little Miss Law and Order, always ready to follow the rules.

"Let him in."

Charlie was halfway in the door before I finished my sentence.

"Hey, Sunshine. You're not superstitious, are you?" He folded me in his embrace.

"No. We make our own luck, good or bad."

About that time, Rayna and Alex ran in yammering that it was time to get married. Charlie and I had decided to include the kids in our wedding vows, and they were thrilled. They were both excited about having a sibling, and all in all, we made a great family.

Sometime in the next couple of years, we planned to build a house on Charlie's land by the old dam. That seemed a fitting way to complete the circle of our lives.

"I'm so happy I'm about to bust." That was the understatement of the century. Our new family was a wonderful collage of personalities. I was even grateful for Bucky. Particularly since, as a judge, he'd be performing our ceremony. Now all I had to do was concentrate on marrying my soul mate.

"So, kiss me!" I said.

He grinned. "I can do that." Boy, did he ever.

And I knew, with everything in me, that my destiny was to love Charlie, summer after summer.

* * * * *

REQUEST YOUR FREE BOOKS!
2 FREE NOVELS PLUS 2 FREE GIFTS!

H HARLEQUIN®

super romance®

More Story...More Romance

YES! Please send me 2 FREE Harlequin® Superromance® novels and my 2 FREE gifts (gifts are worth about $10). After receiving them, if I don't wish to receive any more books, I can return the shipping statement marked "cancel." If I don't cancel, I will receive 6 brand-new novels every month and be billed just $4.94 per book in the U.S. or $5.24 per book in Canada. That's a savings of at least 14% off the cover price! It's quite a bargain! Shipping and handling is just 50¢ per book in the U.S. and 75¢ per book in Canada.* I understand that accepting the 2 free books and gifts places me under no obligation to buy anything. I can always return a shipment and cancel at any time. Even if I never buy another book, the two free books and gifts are mine to keep forever.

135/336 HDN F47C

Name _____ (PLEASE PRINT) _____

Address _____ Apt. # _____

City _____ State/Prov. _____ Zip/Postal Code _____

Signature (if under 18, a parent or guardian must sign)

Mail to the **Harlequin® Reader Service:**
IN U.S.A.: P.O. Box 1867, Buffalo, NY 14240-1867
IN CANADA: P.O. Box 609, Fort Erie, Ontario L2A 5X3

Are you a current subscriber to Harlequin Superromance books and want to receive the larger-print edition?
Call 1-800-873-8635 or visit www.ReaderService.com.

* Terms and prices subject to change without notice. Prices do not include applicable taxes. Sales tax applicable in N.Y. Canadian residents will be charged applicable taxes. Offer not valid in Quebec. This offer is limited to one order per household. Not valid for current subscribers to Harlequin Superromance books. All orders subject to credit approval. Credit or debit balances in a customer's account(s) may be offset by any other outstanding balance owed by or to the customer. Please allow 4 to 6 weeks for delivery. Offer available while quantities last.

Your Privacy—The Harlequin® Reader Service is committed to protecting your privacy. Our Privacy Policy is available online at www.ReaderService.com or upon request from the Harlequin Reader Service.

We make a portion of our mailing list available to reputable third parties that offer products we believe may interest you. If you prefer that we not exchange your name with third parties, or if you wish to clarify or modify your communication preferences, please visit us at www.ReaderService.com/consumerschoice or write to us at Harlequin Reader Service Preference Service, P.O. Box 9062, Buffalo, NY 14269. Include your complete name and address.

HSRDIR13R

REQUEST YOUR FREE BOOKS!
2 FREE NOVELS PLUS 2 FREE GIFTS!

HARLEQUIN®

SPECIAL EDITION

Life, Love & Family

YES! Please send me 2 FREE Harlequin® Special Edition novels and my 2 FREE gifts (gifts are worth about $10). After receiving them, if I don't wish to receive any more books, I can return the shipping statement marked "cancel." If I don't cancel, I will receive 6 brand-new novels every month and be billed just $4.74 per book in the U.S. or $5.24 per book in Canada. That's a savings of at least 14% off the cover price! It's quite a bargain! Shipping and handling is just 50¢ per book in the U.S. and 75¢ per book in Canada.* I understand that accepting the 2 free books and gifts places me under no obligation to buy anything. I can always return a shipment and cancel at any time. Even if I never buy another book, the two free books and gifts are mine to keep forever.

235/335 HDN F46C

Name	(PLEASE PRINT)

Address		Apt. #

City	State/Prov.	Zip/Postal Code

Signature (if under 18, a parent or guardian must sign)

Mail to the Harlequin® Reader Service:
IN U.S.A.: P.O. Box 1867, Buffalo, NY 14240-1867
IN CANADA: P.O. Box 609, Fort Erie, Ontario L2A 5X3

Want to try two free books from another line?
Call 1-800-873-8635 or visit www.ReaderService.com.

* Terms and prices subject to change without notice. Prices do not include applicable taxes. Sales tax applicable in N.Y. Canadian residents will be charged applicable taxes. Offer not valid in Quebec. This offer is limited to one order per household. Not valid for current subscribers to Harlequin Special Edition books. All orders subject to credit approval. Credit or debit balances in a customer's account(s) may be offset by any other outstanding balance owed by or to the customer. Please allow 4 to 6 weeks for delivery. Offer available while quantities last.

Your Privacy—The Harlequin® Reader Service is committed to protecting your privacy. Our Privacy Policy is available online at www.ReaderService.com or upon request from the Harlequin Reader Service.

We make a portion of our mailing list available to reputable third parties that offer products we believe may interest you. If you prefer that we not exchange your name with third parties, or if you wish to clarify or modify your communication preferences, please visit us at www.ReaderService.com/consumerschoice or write to us at Harlequin Reader Service Preference Service, P.O. Box 9062, Buffalo, NY 14269. Include your complete name and address.

HSEDIR13R

REQUEST YOUR FREE BOOKS!

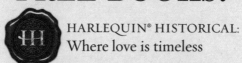

HARLEQUIN® HISTORICAL:
Where love is timeless

2 FREE NOVELS PLUS 2 **FREE GIFTS!**

YES! Please send me 2 FREE Harlequin® Historical novels and my 2 FREE gifts (gifts are worth about $10). After receiving them, if I don't wish to receive any more books, I can return the shipping statement marked "cancel." If I don't cancel, I will receive 6 brand-new novels every month and be billed just $5.44 per book in the U.S. or $5.74 per book in Canada. That's a savings of at least 16% off the cover price! It's quite a bargain! Shipping and handling is just 50¢ per book in the U.S. and 75¢ per book in Canada.* I understand that accepting the 2 free books and gifts places me under no obligation to buy anything. I can always return a shipment and cancel at any time. Even if I never buy another book, the two free books and gifts are mine to keep forever.

246/349 HDN F42C

Name	(PLEASE PRINT)	
Address		Apt. #
City	State/Prov.	Zip/Postal Code

Signature (if under 18, a parent or guardian must sign)

Mail to the **Harlequin® Reader Service:**
IN U.S.A.: P.O. Box 1867, Buffalo, NY 14240-1867
IN CANADA: P.O. Box 609, Fort Erie, Ontario L2A 5X3

Want to try two free books from another line?
Call 1-800-873-8635 or visit www.ReaderService.com.

* Terms and prices subject to change without notice. Prices do not include applicable taxes. Sales tax applicable in N.Y. Canadian residents will be charged applicable taxes. Offer not valid in Quebec. This offer is limited to one order per household. Not valid for current subscribers to Harlequin Historical books. All orders subject to credit approval. Credit or debit balances in a customer's account(s) may be offset by any other outstanding balance owed by or to the customer. Please allow 4 to 6 weeks for delivery. Offer available while quantities last.

HHDIRI3R